The Steel Angel

Center Point
Large Print

Also by Ray Hogan and available from
Center Point Large Print:

Wanted: Dead or Alive
Panhandle Gunman

**This Large Print Book carries the
Seal of Approval of N.A.V.H.**

THE Steel Angel

RAY HOGAN

CENTER POINT LARGE PRINT
THORNDIKE, MAINE

This Circle Ⓥ Western is published by
Center Point Large Print in the year 2016 in
co-operation with Golden West Literary Agency.

August, 2016
First Edition

Printed in the United States of America
on permanent paper.
Set in 16-point Times New Roman type.

ISBN: 978-1-68324-078-5

Library of Congress Cataloging-in-Publication Data

Names: Hogan, Ray, 1908–1998, author.
Title: The steel angel / Ray Hogan.
Description: First edition. | Thorndike, Maine : Center Point Large Print,
2016. | Series: A Circle V western
Identifiers: LCCN 2016015289 | ISBN 9781683240785
   (hardcover : alk. paper)
Subjects: LCSH: Large type books. | GSAFD: Western stories.
Classification: LCC PS3558.O3473 S74 2016 | DDC 813/.54—dc23
LC record available at https://lccn.loc.gov/2016015289

Chapter One

"Where the hell is he?" Joe Denver said.

Standing at the edge of the water, Adam Rait stared out across the restless surface of the Gulf. He could barely make out the freighter lying offshore, its rigging scratched blackly against a sullen night sky. That it was the ship chartered by Kurt Hanover he was dead certain, and he was equally certain that he had brought his crew of hard-bitten teamsters to the correct point of rendezvous.

He recalled Kurt Hanover's words: *Thirty miles upcoast from Galveston . . . and be god-damned sure you're there, ready to pull out.* And his answer: *I'll be there. Not so sure you'll be. Yankee gunboats have got the Gulf locked in tight.* Whereupon Hanover, portly, deceptively genial, chomping on his black Havana cigar, had grinned and said: *Leave the Yankees to me. Never yet met a man who couldn't be bought.*

"You figure that's him out there?" Denver asked, again breaking the hush. "The boys are getting a mite jumpy . . . all this damn' stalling around."

"Let 'em!" Rait snapped. "They're drawing pay for it."

"It's that Gannon, mostly. Shooting off his mouth all the time. He's trouble."

5

"Maybe so, but I was looking to hire the best teamsters on the road. And he's one of them."

"Ain't arguing the fact," Denver said in a dry, dissatisfied way, "but you sure could've looked under a lot of rocks and not found nothing like him."

Adam shrugged. He guessed he couldn't blame the crew for getting edgy. For three nights running they had gathered in the clammy darkness along the Texas coast and waited futilely for Kurt Hanover. Sure, they were getting paid for it—well paid. But it takes more than that to satisfy a man; he needs to know what it's all about—and why.

Perhaps this would be the night. A heavy overcast smothered the stars and visibility was next to nothing. It would require just such celestial assistance for Hanover to slip successfully through the Yankee blockade.

A faint clanking sound drifted across the water from the ship. Immediately Denver moved to Rait's side. "What was that?"

"Could be starting to unload now," Adam replied, relieved. He glanced to the west. "They'd better ease off or that racket'll be heard clear up to the bay."

"Reckon I ought to bring down the teams?"

"Not yet. Better they stay hidden in the brush in case a patrol boat comes along. Saw a light off the point there a while ago."

Turning, he looked toward the thick stand of brush and trees where he had established a camp. Everything was in order—he had checked and rechecked.

Twenty-four experienced teamsters, forty horses, twenty-four of which were now in harness, ready to hitch onto the twelve wagons Hanover was bringing in. A cook, a swamper, a hostler to look after the remuda, a chuck wagon, a light rig for gear, and a saddle horse apiece for Hanover and himself. The only thing undecided was the amount of trail supplies; Kurt had never got around to telling him where they were going or exactly how long they would be on the road.

Rait had followed the man's instructions to the letter, and he was ready. All that was lacking was Hanover—and the mysterious cargo they were to move.

Like Denver and the other teamsters, he had wondered about the cargo, but he had not permitted it to trouble him. To Adam Rait it was just a job, and he'd know what it was all about eventually. What interested him most was that he would get $500 in Yankee gold for assembling and bossing the wagon train—and in the spring of 1865, that was a lot of money.

The son of a Tennessee farmer and his school-teacher wife, he had done his share toward grubbing out a living from eighty hard-rock acres until a fire had taken the lives of both his parents and cut him adrift. A job here and there, several years in Mexico, and then the war had come along, and he had joined with Nathan Forrest and his Confederate cavalry. Three years later he was a wounded captain in a Georgia hospital where they had dug an apple-sized chunk of shrapnel from his thigh.

In June of 1864, limping, frustrated, and haunted by the recollection of men who had died under his command, seemingly for no purpose, he had wanted but one thing from the Army—out. His request had been granted.

More noise was coming from the freighter—dry thuds, clankings, the muted squeal of pulleys. Adam glanced to the sky. The overcast appeared to be breaking up. Hanover had better hurry.

One of the horses blew gustily and stamped a newly shod hoof. Trace chains rattled, and a teamster swore graphically. Toward Galveston, Rait could see more lights on the water, crawling slowly through the murk. Patrol boats, he guessed, venturing forth to investigate the sounds. He felt the sudden press of tension but brushed it away. Kurt Hanover was capable of taking care of himself.

Rait hadn't cared much for the man at their first meeting. They had come together in Huntsville, then a sort of junction point for several passenger and freight lines. Rait had found a job there after he had quit the Army as an agent for one of the outfits. Agent—the title covered a broad range of duties. He was obliged not only to sell fares and look after the needs of passengers, along with the handling of freight shipments, but he served also as hostler, blacksmith, reserve driver, and occasionally shotgun messenger. About the only chores he didn't perform were those of cooking and cleaning stable.

It was a poor existence for a man of his capabilities, but he didn't object, or even really care. Lonely, deserted by purpose, scarred in mind by the things he had looked upon during the war, in body by actual conflict, it was the ideal prosaic world he had sought for, in which he could shoulder a minimum of responsibility.

Kurt Hanover had come onto the scene some three months after Rait had established himself in Huntsville. Well dressed in hard-to-get broadcloth, a cigar thrusting jauntily from the corner of his mouth, he had stepped from an east-bound coach one hot morning, hooked thumbs in his vest armholes, and glanced about in a sharp, perceptive manner.

Adam noticed him as he led out the change team and began to back them into position. Sweat flanked the man's cheeks, and he had mentally observed that it was a hell of a hot day to go around dressed up like a schoolteacher playing Santa Claus.

"You Rait?" the pilgrim had asked unexpectedly.

Suspicious of the man, Adam had paused to take a second look. Another slicker aiming to give somebody a fast shuffle, he had decided. "Could be," he grunted.

"Friend of yours told me to see you. I'm Hanover, Kurt Hanover."

Adam resumed his hitching. "What friend?"

"A major . . . name of Bowman . . . Missouri cavalry."

Again Rait hesitated. Bowman had, at one time, been his commanding officer. There had been no particular rapport between them other than that existing between officers of different rank. He was surprised that Bowman even remembered him.

"Why . . . ," he began, then became aware of the driver's impatient glare. "Be through here in a minute," he said.

Hanover rocked on his heels, toyed with a heavy gold chain looped across his slight paunch. "Can you put me up for the night? Got a proposition to make you."

Rait spat. Just as he'd figured, a slicker. "Big money in it for me, I suppose?" he drawled, beginning his usual check of pins, single-tree U-bolts, buckles, and chains.

Hanover nodded. "Plenty. How about that bed?"

"I think I can find room for you."

The stage pulled out, leaving the two men

standing in the dust and sweltering heat of a Huntsville morning. Adam led the way into the clapboard station where it was no cooler. He pointed to a chair and settled himself on the edge of a table that served as a desk.

Unhurried, Hanover removed his coat, unbuttoned his vest. Opening a silver case, he offered a cigar to Adam, selected a fresh one for himself. "We alone?"

Rait bit off the end of the weed, searched his pockets for a match. "Cook in back, stable boy outside."

"Blacks?"

"Mexicans. Negroes all ran off, looking for that freedom the Yankees promised them."

"Good. Can't trust them nowadays anyway."

You could before the Yankees came busting into the South filling their heads with crazy notions, Adam thought, lighting his cigar, but that was neither here nor there. Exhaling, he stared at Hanover through the smoke and waited for him to speak.

"Your friend . . . Bowman . . . put me onto you. Said you were a good man." Kurt Hanover, at ease, leaned back in his chair. "Fact is, he said you were the best he'd ever seen when it come to handling men and horses. Happens to be just what I'm looking for . . . if you've got a fair knowledge of the country."

"Texas?"

Hanover nodded.

Adam removed his cigar, studied the glowing end. "This got something to do with the Army?"

"Not necessarily."

Rait shrugged. "Had my fill of soldiering, you know."

"Can't say as I blame you. Far as I'm concerned a man's a damned fool to get himself all frizzed up in a shooting war. No offense, you understand, I just never could see any sense in risking your neck for nothing."

Adam made no reply, preferring not to reopen any wounds.

"Anyway, the Army as such doesn't concern us. I'm only asking if you're acquainted with the country."

"Born in Tennessee, but I've knocked around Texas pretty well."

"Good. Seems Bowman was right, so far. Now here's what I'm needing . . . teamsters, horses, chuck and supply wagons, and all the necessary items and equipment to make up a train of which you would be wagon master. Two thousand dollars would be deposited in the Huntsville bank. You would draw against the account for purchasing and hiring. Everything is to be ready and waiting at a specified point on the coast at a time I'll tell you later."

Adam Rait wasn't interested. The weight of command was still a repelling memory stamped indelibly in his mind: men relying upon his judgment, men bowing to his orders, men dying. . . .

"Count me out. Not interested."

"Not for five hundred dollars . . . gold?"

Adam stirred. It was a lot of money, and he had given some thought to drifting on West if ever he could get a little cash together.

"Won't be much responsibility," Hanover said, sizing up the reluctance correctly. "Once I've put in with the cargo, I'll be looking after things. All I'm asking you to do is the hiring and the buying up of the livestock . . . getting things ready."

"Why don't you do it yourself?" Rait asked.

"Well, I'm a fair judge of men, but I'm no horse trader, and I admit it. Mainly I won't be around. I've got some buying to do, shipping to arrange. Just want you to have everything set when I get here."

"How long'll that take?"

"Several months. Be plenty of time for you to line up the best teamsters in the country and do your horse buying."

"What about wagons?"

"Won't need wagons. I'll be bringing my own. You pick us up one for the cook and one to haul supplies in."

Adam had asked a few more questions and finally agreed. In the months that followed

13

during which he had assembled the train, he had wondered several times what it was all about. That it involved blockade running was evident. But with what and for whom was as yet undetermined.

He hoped it was nothing detrimental to the Confederacy; a spark or two of loyalty for the Glorious Cause still glowed somewhere within him, although he had long since convinced himself that it was lost. Gettysburg had been the turning point. But the leaders of the Confederacy had been too stump-headed to admit it.

"Fog's moving in."

At Denver's remark, Adam came back to the moment. He nodded to the square-built man he had selected to be teamster boss. "It'd be a help."

He looked for the freighter. It was no longer visible, wholly swallowed up by the thickening mist. Somewhere to the north a bell tolled, and farther out a horn moaned, desolate and lonely. Rait frowned, thinking that the fog could work both ways. While it would mask the activities of the ship, it could also make it difficult for Hanover—if Hanover it was—to locate them.

Denver had a similar thought. "Maybe we ought to be lighting up a bonfire."

Adam started to reply but caught himself, some inborn instinct plucking at his consciousness, sending a warning racing through him. He wheeled, threw a glance at a band of shadowy brush below the camp. Someone was watching them. He felt it, was sure of it, although he could see no one. Touching the butt of the pistol at his hip, he was about to cross over and investigate.

Almost immediately a voice from the thick curtain lying upon the water cried guardedly: "Hello, the shore!"

Adam came around swiftly. It was Hanover—at least he thought so. Certainly no seafaring man would have hailed them with those words.

"Here!" he called, cupping his hands to his mouth. "Hanover?"

"Sure is," the reply drifted back.

Chapter Two

For a few moments there was only the quiet swish of oars coming from the mist, and then Hanover's voice again.

"Teams ready?"

"Ready and waiting."

"Good. Got the first wagon floating behind us. Rest'll be following."

"Floating?" Joe Denver muttered. "What kind of rig's he talking about?"

Adam wondered, too, but from Kurt Hanover you could expect anything. "Bring down the teams," he told Denver.

Denver stamped away on his stumpy legs, still talking to himself. Rait glanced again to the brush below camp, intuition unsatisfied, saw nothing, and moved to the edge of the water. He peered into the murk. Abruptly the bow of a dinghy poked its nose through the damp veil.

Hanover, hands braced against the gunnels, was staring straight ahead. He saw Adam and settled back, sighing audibly. "Plenty glad to see you, mister."

Rait waded out to knee depth, grasped the ring on the prow of the small boat, and dragged it to the low bank.

Kurt, dressed in coarse woolens and wearing an

oilskin coat and cap, leaped ashore. He grinned broadly, extending his hand. "Everything go all right for you?"

"Just the way it was supposed to," Adam replied, looking beyond the dinghy and the two sailors resting on their oars. "You say something about a wagon?"

"Bringing in twelve, and all of 'em loaded," Hanover said.

The first of the teams was moving up; the horses were pawing nervously in the darkness, setting their harness metal to jingling. Denver sawed them to a halt, looked expectantly at Hanover.

Adam bobbed his head at the driver. "My lead teamster, Joe Denver."

Hanover nodded, turned to the dinghy. "All right, boys, swing her in," he said, and beckoned to Rait.

The seaman in the stern of the craft turned half about, picked up a hawser, and began to tug at it. His companion, pushing the prow free of the shore, paddled the craft to one side, clearing the way.

Hanover said: "Tongue's been removed from the wagons. We'll float them in close, tie on ropes, and drag them onto land with the horses." He paused, looked to the eastern sky. "Got to work fast. I want everything back in the trees out of sight before sunup."

Adam wondered again, briefly, as to the nature

of the cargo being transported, and also how a loaded vehicle could be floated successfully. He was face to face with part of the answer in that next moment.

A narrow, elongated, box-like contraption broke through the fog, sluggishly drifting toward him. Water glistened on the oilskin wrappings of its contents, and the dull shine of metal tires, exceptionally wide, flickered as the wheels bobbed up and down on the surface.

To the sides of the wagon bed, like broad, full-length mudguards, thick planks had been affixed at right angles forming crude but effective pontoons. Thus, the water-tight, wheeled box with its wings provided a buoyancy that easily supported itself and its contents.

"H'yars your hawser," one of the sailors said, and flung the coil at Hanover.

"Won't need it," Adam said, sizing up the arrangement. He motioned to Denver and waded out to meet the wagon. "Swing your team around, and toss me the traces."

Denver wheeled his brace, grabbed the trailing leather straps and chains, and then backed the nervous horses to the edge of the water. Still clutching the reins, he passed the traces to Adam, now holding to the forward edge of the wagon bed to prevent its drifting off.

Releasing his grasp, Rait turned the traces sideways, placed the iron rings on the tongue bracket, and dropped the pin into place. "Drag it out," he told Denver.

Denver slapped leather to his horses, sent them lunging forward. The wagon surged toward the shoreline, sending a foot-high wave rushing ahead of it, and halted abruptly.

"Against a mud bank!" Adam shouted. "Double team it."

Behind him he could hear the steady slice of oars again. A second boat, bringing in another wagon was almost there.

"Come on, come on!" Hanover said impatiently. "Things are going to pile up here if we ain't careful."

"Ready," Joe Denver said from the darkness.

Adam moved away from the wagon. A whip popped hollowly. Denver's strident voice shouted—"Git, you hump-nosed glue farms!"— and the wagon lurched forward. Its front wheels struck the underwater ledge, stalled momentarily, and then rolled on. Shortly it was on dry land, water pouring from it in a hundred cascading rivulets.

After the first it was easy. The bank quickly wore down to a slope and the teamsters were not long in getting the hang of maneuvering the odd, heavily loaded vehicles. By the time the first flare of sunrise was brightening the east, the last was ashore, the dinghies had departed into the mist, and the train was almost ready to move.

Hanover, as wet to the skin as was Rait, rubbed his hands together and grinned. "Made it . . . and just in time. Where's camp?"

Adam pointed to the grove a hundred yards distant. "Cook'll have some grub waiting. Only thing that's still undone is laying in a full supply for the trip."

Hanover expressed annoyance, "You were supposed to be all ready!"

"Would have had that done, too, only you never got around to telling me how long we'd be on the road."

"Important we move out today."

"We will. Town's about two miles off. I'll take the cook and buy what we'll be needing and catch up. There'll be no time lost." There was a sharp edge to Adam Rait's voice.

Hanover grinned, slapped him on the shoulder. "Sure thing."

Adam raised his arm to give Joe Denver a signal. Immediately the lead wagon sprang into motion and began to move toward the camp. He turned back to Hanover. The blockade runner was staring off to their left at an approaching buggy in which sat a lone man.

"How long you been here?" Hanover asked anxiously.

"Three days," Adam informed him.

Kurt swore quietly. "Expect whoever that is has been sitting there, watching you all the time."

Adam glanced to the right at the brush that had drawn his attention earlier. "Had a feeling somebody was . . . but not from that side of the cove."

Chapter Three

Hanover looked at Rait questioningly. He started to speak but thought better of it and swung his attention back to the approaching buggy.

The driver pulled to a halt and climbed down hastily. He was a Mexican, conservatively dressed in dark gray suit and a black plug hat. He stood for a moment with his eyes on the freighters moving toward the grove, and then faced the two men. Fog had begun to lift slightly, but there was still a thin mist; silhouetted against the brassy flare in the east, the visitor appeared strange and unreal.

"I am Emiliano Escobar," he said in the precise style of foreigners who have been carefully tutored in an unfamiliar language. "Which of you is Mister Hanover?"

"Me," Kurt replied bluntly, reaching for his cigar case. His hand fell away when he remembered he had left the container in his jacket.

"And you?" Escobar asked politely, glancing at Rait.

"Adam Rait."

"A pleasure, gentlemen." The Mexican looked again at the train. Half the vehicles had reached the grove and were out of sight in the dense brush and trees. "You bring a large cargo, Mister Hanover."

"So?"

"It is of extreme, and even vital, interest to those I represent."

"Who's that?" Hanover asked.

Escobar hesitated as Joe Denver came trotting up. The squat teamster's broad face was lined into a deep frown. "We pulling out, or we staying the night?"

"We're pulling out," Hanover answered before Adam could speak. "Right away."

Denver bobbed his head, wheeled, and headed back for camp.

Escobar began: "I represent *Presidente* Benito Juárez and the Republic of Mexico."

Hanover merely nodded, but Adam looked more closely at the quiet-faced man. He was a Juárista, and a long way from headquarters.

"Your cargo . . . it can be purchased?" Escobar asked.

Hanover shrugged. "Usually anything I own's for sale."

The Mexican took an eager half step forward. "It is possible then to negotiate?"

"Afraid not, *señor*. It's already sold. Deal was made before I ever went after it," Hanover explained.

Escobar's face sagged with disappointment. "I have waited many days, hoping . . . is it possible you can be persuaded to a change of mind?"

Kurt Hanover shook his head. "One thing I've

never done is gone back on a deal . . . and I won't start now. It's bad for business." He paused, then added: "Tell you this . . . once I get this shipment delivered, I'll be ready to talk turkey."

"Talk turkey?" Escobar repeated wonderingly, and then said: "Yes, I understand. Such would require many months, is that not so?"

"To make delivery to you? Be close to a year . . . that's if my luck holds."

"I fear that would be too late," Escobar said quietly.

Hanover glanced longingly toward the camp and the dry clothing and black cigar that awaited him there. "Best I could do. How goes your revolution, *señor*?"

"It has not yet reached full proportions. The *presidente* remains in hiding, but we are informed by reliable sources in Mexico City that soon the French Emperor will withdraw his army, leaving Maximilian to cope unaided with his problems."

"Ought to be just what you're looking for."

"Indeed. At such time we hope to strike. We strive now to have everything in readiness, for without the French soldiers to fight for Maximilian, our chances for overthrowing him and restoring the people's republic will be excellent . . . but we must have arms and ammunition with which to do this."

Adam Rait settled back. So that was what

Hanover was engaged in—gunrunning. Rifles and ammunition. He should have known the moment he saw the long wooden cases in their waterproof wrappings, the specially built wagons with their heavy axles and wide-tread wheels. He wondered then who the purchaser of the shipment could be? Maximilian? It would be like Hanover to sell to the Mexican Emperor, and immediately turn around and sell also to the opposing Juáristas. But it couldn't be Maximilian and Mexico. Hanover had questioned him as to his knowledge of Texas. . . .

"Sure like to help," Kurt was saying briskly, watching the last wagon disappear into the trees. "But I would if I could. And you can believe that. Always kind of liked your Benito Juárez."

Like most Americans he pronounced the displaced *presidente*'s name war-*ezz*, with the accent on the last syllable.

"You look favorably on our struggle for right?" Escobar brightened.

"Sure. I think the Mexican people got a raw deal. Juárez is a good man."

"Then perhaps it would be possible to negotiate for half your cargo? What value would you set on such a portion?"

"Twenty thousand dollars . . . but it's no deal, *señor*. Still aim to stand by my agreement . . . and my customer is waiting. Like I said, once I've taken care of them, I'll make a trip to Juárez

25

City and have a talk with your *presidente*. Maybe it won't be too late."

Emiliano Escobar lowered his head in defeat. "Very well, Mister Hanover. I can do no more." He shook hands gravely with both men and turned to his buggy. Pausing there, he said: "Should there be change and you wish to again meet with me, I may be found in Galveston, at the home of a friend, *Don* Francisco Chavez. *Vaya con Dios, amigos*."

Hanover nodded.

Rait said: "*Adiós, señor*." He felt a tinge of sadness for the little man. That the patriots of Mexico needed help was common knowledge. Again he pondered the destination of Hanover's cargo and decided that if by some chance it was to go, ultimately, to Maximilian, he'd call it quits, go back to Huntsville, and see if his old job was still open. He was no flag waver, but the way Napoleon III had jammed the Austrian Archduke down the throats of the Mexican people was enough to gag anyone.

"Sort of like to help him," Hanover said as they watched the buggy roll away. "But gold's gold, and I'm a man to stick with my agreement." He looked at Adam. "Expect you know now what this's all about."

"I know we're freighting rifles and ammunition. What I don't know is who for?"

"The Confederacy."

"The Confederacy!" Rait echoed in surprise. He stared at Kurt. "Where the hell's the Confederacy going to get forty thousand dollars in gold?"

"They've got it . . . leastwise the bunch I made a deal with have. Made sure of that before I ever shipped out for Germany."

Adam shook his head. "There's been a lot happening since you left. Might be better to deal with the Mexicans."

"I'll deal with them later . . . after I've collected for this load. What do you mean a lot's happened?"

"The South's lost the war. Grant's got Lee backed against a wall with no place to go. The Confederacy's going on guts and nothing else. They just don't have sense enough to give in."

Hanover looked sharply at Rait. "Was a time when you didn't think that way, I'm told."

"Right," Adam said mildly. "Then I woke up to the fact that a lot of men were getting killed for no good reason . . . and I was a part of it."

"Fortunately the jaspers I'm dealing with don't look at it that way," Hanover said. "I'm damn' glad of it . . . forty thousand dollars' worth of glad. Come on. I want to get into some dry clothes."

As they started for the camp, Kurt asked: "Seen any soldiers around, Confederate or otherwise?"

"None. Had a feeling somebody was watching us from the brush early this morning. Could've been wrong."

27

"Some pot-licker from town, probably," Hanover decided, dismissing the report.

"Where are we taking this shipment?" Rait asked. "You never got around to telling me."

"Didn't figure it was important to you," the experienced blockade runner replied, "but we're headed for Marshall."

"Who's there? Kirby Smith's across the line in Shreveport, but I don't remember hearing anything about any soldiers in Marshall."

Hanover shrugged. "All I know is that I make delivery there, and collect my money. Plenty of high-ups are in on the proposition."

"Smith?"

"Him I wouldn't know about for sure, and I don't give a damn. Rule of mine is to never look under the bed to see who's hiding. I just take my money and go."

Adam Rait reckoned it was no concern of his, either. He was getting $500 in gold for bossing a wagon train to Marshall, and all else was a side issue and shouldn't worry him.

It was dawn, and Sancho, the Mexican cook, had breakfast ready when they reached the square formed by the wagons: beans, side meat, flat corncakes, and a drink that passed for coffee, but just barely. Hanover took one swallow and spat.

"What in the name of God is this?"

Rait grinned. "Roasted acorns pounded to meal. No coffee around anywhere . . . not with those

Yankee gunboats squatting out there in the Gulf."

Hanover spat again, dashed the liquid to the ground. "Better lay in a supply of whiskey," he said. "Man's got to have something fit to drink with his meals. Got some around?"

"No, except maybe a few bottles the teamsters might have. I'll pick up a gallon while I'm in town."

Joe Denver came up, his brow wrinkled. "Floating didn't do them wagons no good. Got to pull the wheels, dab on fresh grease."

Hanover's face darkened with irritation. "Hubs were greased before they were loaded. Why . . . ?"

"Wagons ain't boats," Denver said calmly. "Reckon your grease sort of washed off."

"How long'll it take?" Hanover was impatient.

"Half a day, probably."

"Then get at it!"

Denver glanced at Adam for approval. At Rait's brief nod the teamster spun and walked quickly back to the crew gathered around one of the vehicles.

Hanover handed his empty plate to Felipe, the cook's swamper, and threw a smile at Rait. "Don't mean to be stealing your thunder. You're the boss of this outfit. Guess it just popped out . . . habit."

"All right with me," Adam said disinterestedly. Two wagon masters would easily confuse matters, but if Hanover wanted to take full charge, let him. Adam Rait would still draw his pay.

Kurt reached for his bag, opened it, and then began to strip off his wet clothing. "You mentioned needing supplies. Does the cook know what we ought to get?"

"I'll write him out a list," Rait said.

Hanover nodded. "I was just thinking there's a few things I need, too. How about me running into town with him and you staying on the job to get the wagons ready?"

It was a good idea, Rait thought. He should stay; there appeared to be a little dissension. Bill Gannon was most likely responsible. "I'll get on it," Adam said, and turned to consult with the cook.

When he had finished, Kurt was dressed and stood leaning against one of the wagons, watching the teamsters at work on another. Denver had cut and trimmed a fair-size tree and was employing it as a lever to hoist the heavily loaded vehicle off the ground. While a half a dozen men pressed their weight upon the pole, two others worked hurriedly to remove the wheels.

"Keep them at it," Hanover commanded, moving to join Sancho who waited for him in the supply wagon. "Ought to be back by noon. Be ready to roll."

Adam nodded. "We'll be ready," he said, irritated by the man's tone, and then he dismissed it from his mind. For $500 in gold he guessed he could get along with the devil himself.

Chapter Four

The servicing of the wagons was a job of no small proportion. Nine of the vehicles contained rifles; twenty-seven cases were bedded so firmly and precisely in each that they appeared to be part of the wagon box itself. The remaining three were loaded with cartridges in smaller wooden cases, equally heavy and expertly packed. To empty the freighters would have been impractical and more time-consuming.

Thus, each teamster and his relief driver were assigned the task of doing the actual lubricating chore on their own particular vehicle, while a half dozen or so of the other men, having finished with their units, took turns bearing down on the leverage pole.

It was hot, back-breaking labor, and near noon, Adam, sweat streaming from every pore in his body, turned after cinching a hub nut and called to Joe Denver. "How many to go?"

"Two. Gannon and Waterhouse."

"All right. You work with Waterhouse." He turned and beckoned to Gannon. "Let's get at it, Bill."

Several of the men trailed off after Denver, others moved up beside Rait. Gannon, squatting in the shade where he had apparently been all morning, did not stir.

Anger flared through Adam. Hot and tired, he was in no mood for opposition. He crossed to where the bull-necked teamster was rising to his feet.

"You heard me, Gannon. It's your wagon!"

"Might be, but I ain't no friggin' stable hand. I hired out to drive. . . ."

"You'll do what I tell you . . . and you're being told now to get busy on your wagon."

"The hell with you!" Gannon shouted, his temper rising also. "I'll look after my driving, but no gimpy wagon boss is . . ."

Rait's balled fist hit him hard and clean on the point of his jaw. He staggered, fell against the tree immediately behind him, and sagged briefly. A yell broke from his lips as he struggled upright. "God damn, I've been hoping you'd try that," he said, and plunged forward.

Adam, outweighed by the thick-shouldered teamster, knew he could never out-slug the man in a toe-to-toe match and doubted he could overcome his bull strength. His best chance was to stay clear, cut Gannon to ribbons, wear him down.

He jerked aside as the teamster rushed in and smashed a sharp, downsledging blow to the man's ear. Gannon stumbled and went to his knees, but came up immediately. He wheeled, bumping into several of the crew now gathered in a circle about the two men.

Adam heard Joe Denver say: "Knew this was

coming. Gannon's been asking for trouble ever since we got here."

Rait stared at Gannon, now more cautious as he moved in slowly at a crouch, arms hanging loosely at his sides. Denver was right. Bill had wanted to start something—and this was the time to settle it.

Rait stepped in quickly, unexpectedly. Driving his left into the teamster's nose, he crossed with a right to the head. Gannon paused, swayed uncertainly. Surprised at the effect of the blows, Rait followed up fast with several sharp drives to the head and body, before he pulled back sucking deep for breath.

Gannon, upright by sheer will, watched Adam with glazed, unseeing eyes. He hung motionlessly for several seconds, and then collapsed soundlessly.

A cheer went up from several teamsters. Rait, sweating profusely and still dragging deep for wind, leaned over, retrieved his hat, and faced the crowd.

"Let's get to those wagons," he snapped, temper still glowing in his eyes. "Somebody throw a bucket of water on Gannon. I want him in there doing his share."

He came about, hearing the metallic sound of iron tires slicing into the sandy soil. Hanover and Sancho had returned. The old cook pulled to a halt beside the chuck wagon, climbed down stiffly, and beckoned to Felipe. Together they began to transfer the new stock of foodstuffs to the other vehicle. Hanover remained on the seat, staring vacantly at the sweating teamsters at work. Finally he, too, descended.

Adam saw that Hanover was drunk, noted also that he had purchased a change of clothing. Hanover now wore hard-finished denim pants, a lightweight shirt, and a wide-brimmed, low-crowned hat. A new gun belt, complete with tooled holster and pearl-handled pistol, encircled his waist.

Rait watched the man unsteadily cross the camp; he guessed Hanover had spent his time in town patronizing a saloon and buying personal items while Sancho took care of the supplies.

"Noon," he said, coming to a stop next to Adam. "Seems I recall you saying you'd be ready by noon."

Kurt Hanover was one of those men who, when intoxicated, spoke slowly and with exaggerated care.

"More of a job than I figured," Adam replied. "Be ready in another hour."

"You said noon!"

"All right. I said noon!" Rait barked, suddenly out of patience. "We didn't make it. Now, suppose you get yourself a little sleep while we finish up. It won't take long."

Hanover frowned, wheeled awkwardly, and

walked to the supply wagon. The teamsters, having paused to watch, resumed their labors.

Gannon was now sitting up, thoroughly drenched, his clothing plastered to his thick body. Under Rait's steady gaze he rose, sauntered to where his partner, Red Lester, and several other men worked at his wagon.

Lester paused, glanced to Hanover sprawled beneath a tree. There was invitation in his manner and it was plain he was anxious to take up with Adam where Bill Gannon had left off.

"A god-damned drunk. We going to be nursemaiding him?"

"It's his train," Rait said.

The teamster swore again. "Going to be one hell of a fine trip. Don't even know where we're headed in a jerry-rigged contraption that's got a seat harder'n a whore's heart . . . and lugging a cargo half the state of Texas would lift our hair for. Now we got us a boss so damned drunk he couldn't hit the ground with a bale of hay. Or . . . ,"—Lester stopped to look directly at Adam—"are you still running this outfit?"

"I am," Rait said evenly. "And I've got a couple of things to say to you . . . and you, Gannon. You're both trouble . . . and trouble I can do without. Draw your wages and move on."

Lester straightened up. Gannon rubbed at his neck. The redhead spat. "Hell, ain't no use you getting all riled up."

"You're the one doing the complaining."

"Ain't said nothing nobody else wouldn't, was they to speak up," Lester said contritely. "If it's all the same to you, I'll keep working."

Adam nodded. He couldn't afford to lose either man but things would have to be done his way. He had enough problems with Kurt Hanover. He swung to Gannon. The teamster's face was beginning to swell.

"What about it, Bill? Quit . . . or work and keep your mouth shut? Your choice."

Gannon looked down. "Reckon I'll stay."

Adam turned to Joe Denver. The squat driver grinned. "Like I was telling you, you could've looked under plenty of rocks . . ."

Rait silenced the man with a shake of his head. "Wind it up . . . we're late."

When all was in readiness, with Denver beside him, Adam made a complete check of the vehicles, assured himself that nothing had been over-looked, and then ordered the drivers to their seats.

Denver pointed to Hanover. "You aiming to tie him to the saddle?"

"He can ride with Felipe in the supply wagon. Fix a bed for him in the back."

"I was just thinking . . . with him in the shape he's in it wouldn't hurt none to lay over, get an early start in the morning."

"That'd be what I'd do, but Hanover's in a hurry. We'll give him what he wants."

Denver nodded. "Which way we headed?"

"North . . . for Marshall. Road's east of here. We'll cut straight to it, then swing left."

"Marshall, eh? These guns for the Army?"

"Right."

"Confederate Army?" the teamster said as though unable to believe his ears.

"That's it."

Joe Denver uncoiled his whip, flipped it full length, and the tip spurted dust from a nearby stump. "Well, seems to me somebody's doing a lot of something for nothing, but I reckon I oughtn't fret long as I get paid."

"That's the way I feel about it," Adam replied.

"Who's at Marshall? Kirby Smith ain't . . . unless he's up and moved. Could it be the Missouri cavalry?"

"Possible. Thought they'd gone on to Virginia, however." He swung his glance over the wagons to see that most of the drivers were ready. "Anyway, it's no business of ours. All we have to do is get the wagon train there. Keep it from the crew long as you can, not all of them are Southerners."

"Just what I was thinking. Want me to pull out now?"

"Wait for my signal."

Adam turned back to the camp. Sancho and Felipe, his young swamper, had completed the transfer of the new stock and were putting the last of the gear into the other vehicle.

"We leave," Adam said to the older Mexican in Spanish. "Are you ready?"

Sancho said: "Yes, all is ready. I will drive the kitchen. Does Felipe drive the other or will the *patrón*?"

"It is possible the *patrón* will ride in the rear," Adam said, and crossed to Hanover. Reaching down, he shook the man's shoulder. Kurt sat up with a start.

"Something wrong?"

"Moving out. Can fix you a bed in the supply wagon . . . or you can ride the horse I got for you."

Hanover scrambled to his feet, dusted himself. He had sobered amazingly during the hour or so of sleep he had taken.

"I'll take the saddle," he said, looking out toward the freighters. "What course you taking?"

"Due east for a couple of miles. We hit the road to Marshall there."

"We come close to that town?"

"No, we'll be above it."

"Good. Be smart to miss all the towns we can." Kurt reached for a cigar, jammed it between his lips, and studied the two horses, saddled and waiting in the shade. "Which one's mine?"

"The black."

"Fine . . . fine . . . always like a tall horse," Hanover said, walking off briskly.

Adam watched him for a moment, and then

wheeled to face the train. He raised his arm to let it sweep downward. Immediately Joe Denver, handling the lead team, cracked his long whip and put his wagon into motion. One by one the others rolled in behind him, taking the position they would hold during the remainder of the journey.

Farther over to the left, the wrangler hazed his string of extra horses into a trot, and to the right, clear of the dust already beginning to lift, Sancho and the boy, Felipe, whipped up their teams.

Adam glanced around the camp, saw that nothing remained. Sighing, he crossed to the bay he had picked for himself and mounted the horse. The train, at last, was under way.

Chapter Five

When they reached the road to Marshall, Adam Rait motioned Hanover on and pulled off to the side. He waited there, gave each wagon sharp scrutiny as the shouting teamsters swung their creaking rigs into the twin ruts. The junction accomplished without incident, he glanced to the remuda, and then to where Sancho and Felipe were keeping pace with their vehicles. All were in position. Satisfied, he returned to the head of the column.

"Things going all right?" Hanover asked, shifting on his saddle.

Adam nodded. "Don't look for many miles today. Always a few problems at the start."

"At least we're moving. What kind of road lies ahead?"

"Fair. Some downgrade."

"That'll help."

Rait looked at Hanover thoughtfully. "Will we be late getting the cargo to Marshall?"

"A bit. I told them to expect me around the first of the month. Not missing it by much."

They rode on in silence. Around them the land lay hot and dry, and high overhead a flock of crows was making a quiet, irregular passage. Adam, eyes squinted to minimize the glare, traced the course of the road. It was beginning to curve left and then apparently fell away sharply into a grade. Wheeling, he doubled back to Joe Denver in the lead wagon.

"Slope coming up. Be using your brakes. Try them now."

The teamster nodded and Rait continued on, warning each driver. Bill Gannon was the only one to give him no verbal acknowledgment—but he did test his blocks.

Rait resumed his position next to Kurt Hanover. The train rolled slowly on under its canopy of dust and rumbling thunder.

They drew near the bend. Once more Adam pulled off.

"Keep going!" he called to Hanover. "I'll hold back. Could be trouble."

He was thinking of the heavy loads, single teams, and untried vehicles—a bad combination on a steep grade.

Kurt waved his understanding. He had reached the turn and was now following the ruts angling off and down between two low mounds.

"Rait!"

At Hanover's shout Adam paused. Hanover was motioning for him to come. Immediately Rait spurred the bay forward, but Hanover was already galloping off. Adam rounded the curve and stared. A dozen yards farther, at the foot of the hill, a carriage had overturned.

Rait halted briefly, threw his signal to Denver just reaching the top of the slope. "Pull up! Been an accident!"

"Pull up! Pull up!" the teamster echoed as he hauled back on the leathers and oak blocks began to screech against iron tires.

Adam rushed to the bottom of the hill. Hanover had already dismounted, was striding toward an elegantly dressed young woman standing off to one side. Two men, one also of obvious quality, the other in ordinary work clothing—and both Mexican—were endeavoring to quiet the span of matched sorrels that were hitched to the upset barouche.

Leaving the saddle, Rait hurried to the two men. "Anybody hurt?"

The well-dressed Mexican shook his head. "We are most fortunate. My sister, Angela," he glanced to the girl, "perhaps has bruises. Nothing more."

"Lucky," Adam agreed. Denver and several teamsters were trotting down the grade, curious as to the delay.

"How'd it happen?" Rait queried.

The Mexican shrugged. "Who is to say? Martinez is a driver of much experience . . . yet we still overturned. The road bends. Possibly it is too sharp."

Adam beckoned to the teamsters. "Let's get this out of the way."

Putting their shoulders to the barouche, they

tipped it back onto its wheels. There appeared to be no damage other than displaced cushions and scattered bags and other containers that Martinez began to collect hurriedly.

Rait stood for a time, looking down at the scuff marks in the dry soil. There was something odd about them; the carriage must have come almost to a dead stop before it flipped over. He turned away, guessed that accounted for the lack of injuries and absence of damage . . . still, coming downgrade at a fair speed . . . it would seem . . .

"Rait!"

Adam looked up. Hanover, in the act of escorting the girl to the carriage, was beckoning to him. He circled the vehicle, waited while Kurt handed her to the seat. She had a much lighter skin than her brother, he noted, and was beautiful in a cold, remote way.

Kurt closed the door, touched the brim of his hat, and stepped back. The barouche moved away, and smiling broadly he faced Adam.

"They'll be traveling with us."

Rait stared as disbelief and shock jarred him. "That's a damned fool thing to do . . . let a woman . . ."

"You ever see a woman like her?" Hanover cut in, hearing none of what Adam said. His eyes were glowing, and sweat laid a bright shine on his cheeks.

"You're asking for trouble!" Rait snapped,

trying to get through to the man. "How do you think it'll work out . . . her being around two dozen teamsters, day and night?"

Hanover seemed to recover himself. He turned toward his horse. "Expect she's been around men before."

"Sure, the polite, gentleman kind like her brother, but not a bunch of footloose mule-skinners and bullwhackers on the prod. Keeping them away from her after dark will be a full-time job."

"I'll look after her," Hanover said, mounting. He sat for a moment, watching the drivers stringing back up the slopes to their wagons. "Yes, sir. I'll be doing just that. . . ."

Adam swore quietly in frustration. "What the hell they tying in with us for? Make a lot faster time in the barouche alone."

"Girl said she was afraid . . . soldiers and road agents, and so on. Her brother's a sick man. They're on their way to Fort Worth . . . want to stay with us far as we go."

"That'll be Marshall," Rait said, more to himself than Kurt. There was some risk on the road, he had to admit—but that didn't help his situation any. Keeping a crew of tough, half-wild teamsters in line would be chore enough without flaunting an attractive woman in their faces twenty-four hours of the day.

"Better change your mind, tell them to go on,"

he said wearily, climbing to the saddle. "Other-wise, look for fireworks . . . starting tonight."

"The lady'll be my problem," Hanover said. "Don't you fret over it. God, Rait, I ain't been around a female like her in months. She'll be worth a lot of trouble."

Adam stared at the man, then turned for the crest of the hill. "Your wagon train," he said. "If you figure it that way, that's how it'll be."

He kept the caravan moving until sundown, and then pulled off the road and made camp in a grove of sycamores. They had covered only a short distance but he had not expected much; it had been more of a trial and getting under way proposition. In the days to come it would be different as he would be striving for a twenty- to thirty-mile minimum.

Hanover remained near the barouche that had halted a distance apart from the freighters. The girl stood by while Martinez, the driver, erected a tent for her use. Adam, moving among the teamsters making his check of livestock and equipment, saw them eyeing her with sharp, speculative interest. He called them together.

"Keep away from that side of the camp," he warned. "Nothing over there for you."

Several of the men laughed and a few remarks were passed at low breath. A voice said: "The boss man's private stuff, that it?"

"Not your concern one way or the other," Rait

snapped. "Now start looking after those horses!"

Joe Denver paused beside him, head cocked slyly. "One good thing, maybe," he said, pointing at Hanover. "She'll be keeping him offen your back for a spell."

Kurt was busy. He hovered over the newcomers like a hen with two chicks, seeing to their needs and comfort and keeping Sancho's helper, Felipe, scurrying around, doing endless small chores, while the old cook grumbled and swore in black Spanish.

The sky was clear, and tarps, carried in the supply wagon in event of rain, were ignored. Blankets were unrolled and placed at the owner's discretion, a teamster generally choosing the spot beneath his own wagon. Relief drivers who had seen no action during the day were assigned sentry duty, each to stand a three-hour watch.

"Who're you feared of?" Bill Gannon asked Rait, already forgetting the altercation he had had with Adam. "Comanch'? Some of our brave soldier boys? Or maybe you just don't want nobody bothering the boss man and the little Mex gal."

Rait studied the teamster coolly. "You learn the hard way, Bill," he said. "I'll be posting guards every night until we get this load delivered."

Gannon started to make a reply but Red Lester took him by the arm, quietly said something, and both men moved away.

Ed Vernon, a lean, bearded man from Ohio

stepped up, broke the tense hush. "Got a horse going lame, Cap'n." He was the only one ever to make any reference to Rait's Army background. "Expect you ought to talk to that wrangler about it."

The pressure within Adam eased. He wheeled, followed Vernon to where the horses were rope-corralled, and made his examination. It was only a minor problem, and after giving Polo instructions as to treatment, Adam returned to the center of camp where Sancho was preparing to dish out the evening meal.

Kurt Hanover elected to remain near the barouche, taking his food with the newcomers; he had Felipe lay out his bedroll not far from the girl's tent. This evoked a string of comments from several teamsters, all of which grew more pertinent when the brother and the driver were seen to climb into the carriage and prepare to sleep.

Adam geared himself for trouble but fortunately it failed to develop. The men had been going for more than eighteen hours and soon all were in their blankets, sleeping soundly.

Hanover, likewise, made no overt moves. Several times during the dark night after the camp had quieted and the fire was dead, Adam, restless, made rounds and not once did he find Kurt missing from his bed. He was being the perfect host, the faithful sentinel.

The cynical streak in Rait said that Hanover was doing his chumming now. Hook comes later. And Hanover would have ample time to land his fish. They were a good twelve days and nights from Marshall.

Chapter Six

They made almost twenty-five miles that next day. The road was good despite the fact it was no main route and they encountered no one except a solitary cowhand, drifting west. Hanover divided his time, spending half riding inside the barouche with the girl and her brother, the rest in the saddle beside Rait.

He was in an expansive mood and talked much about his plans for the future, but as usual, spoke little of the past.

At one point he asked: "You got a family somewhere, Adam?"

Rait shook his head. "I'm the last of it."

"Same here . . . thank God. Nobody to worry about. Was this broomtail to step in a gopher hole tomorrow and break my neck, you'd be the owner of the whole shebang." Hanover grinned, faced Adam squarely. "Sound like good prospects?"

Rait smiled back. "Watch for gopher holes."

"That mean you don't care about having a lot of money?"

"Money's all right. It's the caring for it that bothers me."

"Well, you don't have to worry none. Learned a long time ago to avoid the gopher holes. Plenty of them around . . . not always in the ground."

Kurt's genial manner continued but he said nothing about their guests. He was keeping them—the girl particularly—for himself, Adam figured. One thing he was thankful for. Hanover took great pains to allow no contact between them and the crew.

It came as a surprise, therefore, to Adam when, the third night after camp had been established, Hanover approached him with an invitation to dine with him and the de Aceras.

It was the first time he had heard the name of their fellow travelers, and he stood in silence, thinking of that and wondering at the sudden about-face on the part of Kurt Hanover.

"Thought you ought to be getting acquainted with these people," the blockade runner explained. "I've had the Mex boy pitch me a tent and set up a table. Cook's fixing up something special to eat."

Adam glanced to where the shelter had been erected. It was off by itself, about halfway between the barouche and the chuck wagon— and well outside the camp.

"I'm hardly presentable to dine with a lady," Adam said, not too receptive.

"Spruce up a bit. Razor in my kit. Won't need to do much else."

Hanover was insistent, and Rait finally agreed. Washing himself down from a bucket, he shaved, pulled on clean shirt and pants, and, after seeing to the placement of the sentries, went to Hanover's tent.

The arrangements were elementary. Two planks had been placed side-by-side on wooden boxes and covered by a white cloth to serve as a table. A folding cot and two more boxes were chairs. An unopened bottle of brandy and a lantern graced the center of the spread.

"Not elegant, but practical," Hanover said, uncorking the liquor. He poured a generous measure into a cup for Adam, another for himself. "Luck," he said, and tossed off the drink as though it were water.

It was excellent brandy. Adam felt its warm glow almost before he set his empty cup on the table and realized he must proceed with caution. But there was no time for a second. The entrance to the tent filled suddenly and Hanover's ruddy face broke into a wide friendly smile. Adam turned to meet the visitors.

Kurt bowed deeply. "Mister Rait, I present the *Señorita* Angela de Acera . . . *Señorita*, my wagon master, Adam Rait."

Adam's breath caught. Tall, she had glowing black hair, dark eyes, and a skin like caramel cream. She wore a pale blue dress, cut low in front, and had draped a filmy lace mantilla over her head and around her bare shoulders. Jeweled hoops dangled from her ears, and the yellow light from the lantern glittered against the large gem in a ring on one of her slender fingers.

But there was a coolness to her, a deep reserve that held him at arm's length as she acknowledged the introduction, and he thought: *The name fits . . . Angel of Steel.*

"Her brother, *Señor* Hernando de Acera," Hanover continued.

Rait transferred his attention to the man standing behind Angela. He looked different from the way he had on the road, heavier, and a bit older, perhaps. He was dressed in the conventional grandee-style: slim black pants slit up the sides revealing pure white linen under-drawers, white silk shirt, deep red sash wound around his waist, silver conchos and gold braid decorated his black and red bolero.

"My pleasure, *señor*," Rait said, extending his hand.

Hernando's response was limp. He moved on into the tent, paused while Hanover seated Angela on the cot so she would be next to him.

"Afraid accommodations aren't what you're used to," Kurt said, making his apology.

"It is to be expected," the girl replied, smiling. "One learns to accept when traveling." Her words sounded stiff, unnatural.

Adam stepped to the box at the end of the table, opposite her, sat down. Hernando assumed the one next to Adam. Hanover took up the brandy again and poured. Standing, he lifted his cup, waited until the others did likewise.

"¡*Salud*!"

The three men downed their brandy; Angela merely sipped. Hanover turned then, went to the tent flap, brushed it aside, and shouted: "Sancho! We're ready!"

Adam felt the girl's eyes upon him and looked up at her. She lowered her gaze quickly.

He grinned. "How do you find the trip?"

"Very well."

"Expect you miss the comforts of Mexico City."

The observation appeared to startle her. "I was not aware you knew . . ."

"That you're from there? A guess. I'd hardly expect you to be from anywhere else. I wondered about you traveling without a *duenna*, however. Not customary."

"I am aware of my country's customs," she replied stiffly. "There was no relative available. And where a brother and sister are concerned . . ."

"Another toast!"

Hanover was back at the table, filling the cups again. He lifted his brandy high. "To the most beautiful *señorita* in Mexico . . . and Texas!"

Angela sipped. The men emptied their cups. Hanover seized the bottle by the neck, refilled. "To the *Señor* de Acera. May his health improve!"

Hernando didn't appear to be very sick. Adam followed Angela's example and only took a small swallow. He wished Sancho would come with food. Too much brandy on an empty belly. . . .

Again Kurt Hanover served from the bottle. Rait feigned a swallow while he listened to the man's thickening words that had to do with good luck and good health along the way. Finally Hanover sat down a bit solidly. Conversation lagged, the brunt of what little there was being borne by Hanover. Angela made occasional responses, as did Rait. Hernando remained wholly silent, almost to the point of sullenness; the brandy had hit him hard; his eyes were glazing and his mouth sagged.

Sancho finally appeared with Felipe in tow. They brought tin plates of fried meat, small corncakes, and tart-chopped greens, gathered no doubt along the road that day by the aged cook. There was thick Mexican chocolate to drink—a welcome change for Adam from the bitter coffee substitute. Hanover stayed with the brandy.

The meal brought the occasion to life, and before it was over talk had swung to Mexico and the struggle for power between Maximilian and Benito Juárez.

"The French'll find they got a scrap on their hands," Hanover said, having difficulty with his tongue. "They jus' better be figuring on that."

"It is unjust," Angela said, dabbing at her lips with a small square of lace. "The Mexican people are fortunate to have so noble a man dedicated to their interests. Only he can bring about the reforms that will eliminate ignorance and poverty."

"You are a Royalist, I take it," Adam said, not the least surprised. The *ricos*, enjoying their palatial estates and the luxuries of the court, knew on which side of the bread the butter was spread.

Angela shook her head, setting the jewels in her earrings to twinkling. "I have no politics. I speak only as one who observes."

"Then you ought to be able to see that the Mexican people . . . or the people of any country for that matter . . . should have the right to choose their own government."

Angela's dark brows lifted. The smooth flesh of her shoulders stirred beneath the mantilla. "As I say, I have no politics."

"Way it was meant to be!" Hanover broke in heartily. "Pretty woman's got no business mixing in work that's a man's. More important things she can be doing," he added, fixing his eyes meaningfully upon her.

Angela did not flinch under his leering stare, only smiled.

Hanover reached for the brandy. The bottle was empty. Leaning back precariously, he obtained another from a box at the end of the cot. Pouring a quantity into the girl's cup, he filled his own, and then looked questioningly at Rait.

"Reached my limit," Adam said. "Time I was

excusing myself, anyway. Want to take one more look around camp."

Hanover grinned broadly. "Way he is . . . always watching out for me . . . good man. I was telling him only today he's my heir . . . like a son. Just might end up making him my son." Kurt paused, pointed an unsteady finger at Hernando. "Mind putting the *señor* to bed, Adam? Be doing me and the lady a big favor."

Rait nodded, got to his feet. He glanced at Angela. She seemed to have no intention of leaving. Stepping in behind de Acera, he pulled him upright. Hanover, stumbling over his own boots, made his way to the tent flap, held it back.

Supporting de Acera, Rait murmured his good nights to Angela and Kurt, and then half carried, half dragged Hernando to the barouche. Its door was open and Martinez had already curled up in the forward seat.

Shifting around the Mexican or Spaniard, whichever he was, Adam lifted him onto the cushion and straightened him out as much as possible. Hernando was limp, out cold. He'd feel like all the devils in hell were pounding anvils in his head when morning came and it was time to travel.

Closing the door, Rait turned. Against the wall of Hanover's tent the lantern silhouetted the two occupants. Angela still sat at the makeshift table. Kurt was leaning over her, speaking earnestly.

The blockade runner was losing no time with his young *señorita*, Adam thought, as he moved off through the trees. The camp was asleep and Hernando was dead to the world. He had her all to himself.

But an hour later, when he returned to check the dying embers of the fire, Rait found Angela waiting there.

Chapter Seven

Surprised, Adam threw a glance to Kurt Hanover's tent; the lantern, turned low, still burned. He could see the man seated at the table, elbows crooked, head slung forward. Something had misfired.

Rait crossed to where the girl was staring off into the night. In the pale starlight her skin appeared darker, richer, her eyes much larger.

"Seems you left the *patrón*'s board . . . and bed . . . a mite early," he said, light scorn coloring his tone.

She shrugged. "Your opinion of me is of small consequence." And then in Spanish she added: "The thoughts of a North American dwell always on the pleasures of the body."

"A double pleasure I assure you, my lady," Adam replied, also in the flowery tongue, "when beauty such as yours is encountered. What happened? Was there too much brandy?"

She was staring at him, surprised and startled. "You understood my words?"

"Is it so unusual? You speak English."

"True, but few of your countrymen trouble themselves to learn my language. Yes, there was too much brandy."

"A pity."

"Your pity is for his sake, or mine?"

"For him, perhaps. He made great plans."

She tugged at her mantilla. "You are a grand gentleman," she said icily.

Adam laughed. "Was that not what this was all about? You also had plans. If not, you would have taken leave when I carried your brother to his bed."

"I was aware of my actions."

"I am sure of that. It is unfortunate the brandy was so strong. But do not grieve. There will be other nights."

She studied him coolly. "You have opinions . . . not necessarily correct. What sort of woman do you believe me to be?"

"If I spoke truthfully, you would undoubtedly slap my face."

"Very possibly, because you would be wrong."

"Not likely. I had no difficulty placing you and your brother. A family once rich, now without funds. You seek a return to the good life. A man with much money, such as Hanover . . . although a *gringo* . . . is the answer."

"Again you are mistaken. Money has no meaning."

"I find that difficult to believe. A carriage overturned without reason, in a place where it will be found by a man who hungers for a beautiful woman. . . ."

"Do you think me beautiful, Adam Rait?" she cut in.

The question was so abrupt, so simple and child-like that Adam squirmed. "It would be a lie if I said I did not."

"A thousand thanks. It is a compliment even if it came from you in the manner of a tooth being pulled."

He folded his arms and stared down at her. "There is also another matter . . . I do not think you are Spanish or Mexican, at least wholly. There are words used by you . . ."

"I am half," she said, again cutting him short. "My father is of Spain, a descendant of the conquerors."

"I would believe you grew up in this country."

"New Orleans. I was eighteen when we returned to Mexico City. I say returned because my parents lived there before my birth. Your curiosity is now satisfied?"

He grinned. "Much of it. There is still one thing . . . I am right about Kurt Hanover and his money?"

Angela placed her profile to him. The warmness of the night had placed a faint sheen of moisture on her cheeks. "It is as good a reason as any."

She had finally admitted it. He guessed he should say something to Hanover about it, and then decided the man was old enough to look out for himself.

"I suppose . . . if money is of such great importance."

"There is little today of importance," Angela said heavily. "Everywhere one finds war . . . your country as well as mine. We are all concerned with survival."

"And for survival you are willing to pay any price."

"You speak as would a priest . . . and on this night I have no wish to listen. Walk with me, Adam Rait. I cannot sleep and I am weary of standing."

She turned without waiting for him to agree, moved off into the grove slowly. Adam, the pressures building steadily within him, fell in beside her and for several minutes they strolled in silence through the soft, dappled shadows under the trees. Somewhere in the distance a dove cooed mournfully.

"A lonely cry," Angela murmured. "Do you know about loneliness, Rait? I think not. For men there are always things that can be done."

"A man knows loneliness," Adam replied simply.

"But of a different nature," she said, switching suddenly to English. "It's not the helpless sort of thing a woman faces. A woman is forced to sit by, watch everything that means something fall around her . . . and being helpless can do nothing about it. Can you understand what I'm trying to say?"

"A little."

"Well, it's what I mean. It's a special kind of loneliness, and I don't expect you to understand. No man can. . . ."

She halted beneath a huge chinaberry. Locking hands behind her back, she leaned against the thick trunk, gazed up through an opening in the branches to the star-studded sky.

"A man has his own kind of problems," Rait said. "Guess he just handles them in a different way."

"Meaning he doesn't auction himself off to the highest bidder as a solution . . . as you imply that I'm doing."

"Your words, not mine."

"But your thoughts. What else can a woman offer? She has only herself . . . her body with which to barter."

"She can fall in love with some man, marry, and make a home, have kids."

Angela shook her head. "Not every woman's cut out for that kind of life." She looked squarely at Rait. "Do you think I am?"

He reached out suddenly, seized her by the shoulders, pulled her tight against him. He felt the press of her firm breasts and thighs against him.

"I don't know . . . and maybe don't give a damn," he said in a taut voice, sliding his hands down the curve of her back. "Right now I . . ."

He broke off, feeling the blunt, hard muzzle of a Derringer digging into his belly. Stepping back, he gave her a bleak smile. "You won't need that."

Angela shrugged, and returned the weapon to a pocket in the folds of her dress.

"Seems you don't intend to let anything get in your way."

"You're right, Adam Rait," she answered quietly. "Nothing stands in the way of what I have to do."

Turning, she started back for the camp. Adam watched her retreating figure for several moments, and then followed. When he reached the clearing, she had disappeared into her own tent. He glanced about. All was quiet; even Hanover had forsaken his place at the table and was now sleeping on his cot.

Chapter Eight

Rait was awake long before sunrise. He walked stiffly to the fire where Sancho was throwing together the morning meal, poured himself a cup of coffee. Taking a swallow, he swore, spat what was yet in his mouth, tossed aside the remainder, and again expressed his opinion of the Yankees and their blockade.

Joe Denver and the teamsters were rousing; beginning to hustle the teams into position, they filled the clean hush with a steady run of cursing and sharply echoing slaps. The men were no longer tossing their blankets into the supply wagon, he noted. Now they were folding them to make seat cushions.

He had wondered how long it would take them to solve their discomfort. The vehicles were all hard tails, having been constructed without springs in the interests of a lower point of gravity, and also to avoid a source of breakage under heavy loads. The teamsters had complained continually, but that would cease now.

"The horse Ed Vernon was showing you is lame for sure," Joe Denver said, stepping away from his team and allowing his relief man to finish up. "Reckon there ain't no chance of him coming out of it . . . not with these loads."

"Use one from the remuda," Adam said. "I'll trade him off next town we reach."

"Ain't no horseflesh worth having left in this country," Rube Waterhouse, driver of the column's second wagon, said as he tugged at a trace. The big gray standing half in line did not move. The teamster straightened up. "Back, you slough-footed, slab-sided son-of-a-bitch!" he bellowed in a voice that could have been heard in Galveston.

The horse obediently moved into place. In a calm voice Waterhouse continued: "Like I was saying . . . ain't no decent horseflesh around nowheres. God-damned Army grabbed off every-thing."

Rait nodded agreement, glanced toward the barouche. The team the de Aceras was driving comprised fine examples of excellent, well-bred stock. But they'd never work out on a freighter. They'd pull their hearts out on the first hill. He saw Angela then. She stepped from her tent, paused. Her eyes caught his, locked briefly, and she turned to the carriage.

Immediately Martinez abandoned his job of hitching the team and began to strike the canvas shelter. Hernando, seemingly little worse for wear after the evening's bout with brandy, appeared from the far side of the barouche and took up where the driver had left off.

Adam swung to Denver.

"Any problems besides that horse?"

The teamster shook his head. "Usual brawling going on. Bastards ain't happy 'less they're fighting. And that loose mouth of Gannon's . . ."

"Long as he does his job."

"Sure, sure. Got to admit he's one of the best. Just that consarned yammering of his. Was there a way to sew up his god-damn' . . ."

"¡Señor! ¡Señor! ¡El patrón . . . muerto! Dead!"

Adam Rait spun at the frantic summons. Felipe, eyes wide with fright, was running toward him.

"Who's dead?" he shouted.

"¡El patrón! Mister Hanover. Dead. There is blood! Much blood."

Rait struck out across the camp at a fast run for Hanover's tent. Teamsters, hearing the boy's hysterical cry, rushed to follow. Reaching the shelter, Adam jerked aside the flap, entered. Kurt lay facedown on his cot. A broad stain of dark, crusted blood covered his back.

"Knifed," Denver muttered at his elbow. "Now who the hell would've . . . ?"

Silence followed the teamster's unfinished question, and then Bill Gannon pushed through the jam in front of the tent, grasped Adam by the arm.

"Ain't hard to figure out who done it. One of them greaser friends of his'n. Using a knife, that's their way of killing a man."

Adam knocked his arm away angrily. He pointed to the sheathed Green River at Gannon's belt. "You're carrying a knife. So's about every man here."

"Anybody know who was with him last?" Jules Bundy, one of the relief drivers, asked.

"That gal. Seen her setting in here talking to him."

"He was alive when she left," Rait said. "I saw him sitting at the table alone."

"How about that brother of her'n?"

Adam shook his head. "Dead drunk last night. Put him to bed myself."

Kiowa Jack Green, who had done considerable Indian fighting before turning muleskinner, spoke from the tent's entrance.

"Had me a squint 'round back. Whoever done it snuck in under the canvas. Place where it's been cut loose."

"Any tracks?"

"Nope. Was I asked, I'd say they'd been brushed out."

Adam leaned against the table, eyes on the ground as he tried to think. When he last saw Hanover asleep on his cot, Angela had gone, and Hernando was in the barouche. Of course, either one could have returned later, plunged a blade into Kurt's back—but that didn't seem likely. If what he figured was in the de Aceras' minds was true, Hanover dead would be of no value to them.

"What about that driver . . . Martinez, or

67

whatever his name is?" Kiowa Jack Green wondered.

The same would apply to him, Adam realized. "Count him out. Couldn't have been him."

Bill Gannon spat. "Why? You put him to bed drunk, too?"

"I've got my reasons," Rait said, reluctant for some unaccountable cause to reveal what he felt was the truth concerning the de Aceras. "If you think it's got to be a Mexican, what about Sancho and Felipe? And the wrangler? They're Mexicans, too."

"Hell, it could've been anybody," Joe Denver said. "Maybe even somebody we ain't never seen that's been dogging the train, looking for a chance. Man like Hanover's got plenty of enemies."

"Naw," Bill Gannon said loudly. "Got to be one of them three. That Martinez . . . he's my guess." The teamster whirled, faced the others. "Get a rope, one of you boys. We'll make him own up!"

Rait came around fast. Grabbing Gannon by the shirt front, he slammed him against the table. The boxes overturned, and the husky driver went down in a splintering of wood and tangle of cloth.

"Forget it," he snarled. "Be no lynching while I'm here."

There was a murmur of assent. Bill Gannon picked himself up slowly, went through the motions of dusting himself off. His head was lowered but he never removed his hard glance from Adam. Moving away, he halted in the midst of the men.

"Reckon we're overlooking something? Seen the little Mex filly sort of giving Mister Rait there the eye. Maybe him and Hanover had words."

He got no further. Denver and a tall Virginian named Henry Fox seized him by the arms, spun him about, and shoved him at Lester.

"Get him out of here, Red," Denver growled, "or by Jingo, we'll string *him* up!"

Adam raised his hands for quiet. "Maybe there's more of you feeling that way. I can't prove it wasn't. All I can do is give you my word, I didn't."

"Good enough for us," Rube Waterhouse said promptly. "The question bothering me is what do we do now?"

"We keep going," Adam replied. "Be ready to roll in thirty minutes."

An old driver wearing a dirty strip of cloth diagonally across his face and known as One-Eye Johnson paused in the opening as the others began to drift away.

"Was just wondering . . . with him gone are we going to get paid all the same?"

"You'll get paid," Rait replied. "We'll make delivery of the cargo."

The teamster moved on. Joe Denver remained, his eyes on Hanover. "What'll you do about him? Ain't no town anywheres close, no lawman."

"Bury him," Rait said. He could see no other course to follow. "Have a grave dug back there in the trees, and empty his pockets, put the stuff in a sack for me. I'm going to have a little talk with the de Aceras."

"That means you think maybe they did have something to do with it?"

"I'm not sure what I think, but I'm going to ask a few questions."

In his own mind Adam Rait was fairly well convinced that Hanover's killer had been someone outside the train. Nothing else made sense. But he felt he should do everything possible to get to the bottom of it. Leaving the tent, he crossed to where Angela and Hernando were standing. Both watched him intently. At the rear of the carriage Martinez worked at stowing the luggage.

"You know what I'm here for," he said in blunt English. "Know anything about it?"

Hernando wagged his head sadly. "It is unfortunate. A fine man. A friend."

"See anybody around his tent during the night?"

"No one, *señor*. I . . . I fear I slept most soundly."

Adam shifted his attention to Angela. "And you?"

"He was alive when I last saw him . . . sitting at the table. I heard nothing after I went inside my tent."

70

"You leave it at any time?"

"No."

Rait looked toward Martinez. "What about you, *señor*?" he called in Spanish. "Did you hear or see anyone around the tent of the one who has been slain?"

The driver made a gesture with his hands. "I did not. But then I am one who sleeps well."

Those were the answers he had expected, and he found it illogical to doubt them. They wouldn't murder the man they planned to make their benefactor. The belief that it was someone from the outside strengthened—and whoever he was, he would be far from the scene by now. It was pointless to pursue the matter further.

He started to turn away, halted as Denver came up. The teamster handed Adam a small cloth parcel containing the items removed from Hanover's person, nodded politely to the de Aceras.

Pulling Rait aside, he said: "The little job in the woods is about done. And the wagons are ready. I hear you say we'd keep heading for Marshall?"

"Why not? About all we can do."

"Reckon so. We get there, you can send that stuff of his'n on to his folks. Know where they live?"

"Hanover said he had no relatives."

Denver's eyes spread. "No folks? What're you aiming to do with the money we'll be collecting for the cargo?"

71

The question had already occurred to Adam Rait. He had crawled into his blankets that previous night no more than a wagon master working for a promised fee; he had awakened the next morning with a valuable cargo and a string of freighters on his hands. Hanover had joked about such a situation—had laughingly stated Adam would be his heir—but Rait had considered the declaration a jest. Responsibility. He had made a point of avoiding it. But he had it now—in spades. He came to a reluctant decision.

"I want to talk to the men," he said, and started across the clearing for the wagons.

They gathered quickly, some finishing their interrupted breakfasts, some with only cups of acorn coffee, others merely watchful, dark whiskery faces solemn.

"The freight we're hauling is worth forty thousand dollars . . . delivered," he said, wasting no words on the preliminaries.

"Getting it delivered. That's what we was hired to do," a voice commented. "Who's buying it?"

"The Confederate Army, bivouacked some-where near Marshall."

Rube Waterhouse snorted. "Hell. Confederate money ain't no good!"

"Payment will be made in gold."

"Now, where they going to get . . . ?"

"All of you quit your arguing. Let the man

talk," a lanky teamster broke in angrily. "He's trying to tell us something!"

The murmuring died. Malachi Lee said: "Go ahead, Mister Rait. What're you getting at?"

"Just this. Hanover had no folks. He told me so. That means we've inherited the train . . . cargo and all."

There was a complete silence, and then someone said: "You saying the forty thousand dollars is ours?"

"Looks like it, along with the wagons and livestock. All we've got to do is get delivery made, then we can split, equal share to every man after he's paid the wages he's got coming."

A cheer went up amidst a quick babble of talk. Darby Sims did some hurried calculating, and said: "By damn. We'll be getting better'n a thousand apiece . . . in gold!"

More cheers echoed in the clearing.

Bill Gannon, squatting on his heels, shook his head. "Some kind of a ringer here." He fixed his suspicious eyes on Adam. "You sure you ain't saying this just so's we'll stay on the job. Then when the pay-off's made . . . ?"

"You'll be there with me," Adam said, reading the teamster's thoughts. "You're all part owners. If you don't trust me, send a couple of men along when I collect."

"That's fair enough!" someone shouted.

"All I'm asking is that you help me get the

cargo to Marshall. I figure it's too late to do the South any good, but I could be wrong. There may be some things I don't know. . . ."

"We'll get it there!"

"Then let's get rolling!" Red Lester urged. "Sooner we do, sooner we can start counting out that gold!"

At once the meeting began to break up. Teamsters, ordinarily in no hurry to take up the leathers for a long day's drive, now trotted to their wagons and sprang aboard.

"Rider coming!"

There was a lull in activity. Rait, preparing to mount, threw a glance down the dusty road.

It was a soldier, dressed in faded gray trousers and ragged shirt. A crushed kepi was pulled low on his head. Apparently he was a courier on his way to Marshall, or some other encampment. The Confederate spotted the train and staring men, veered his lathered horse toward the grove.

"War's over!" he cried as he swept by. "Lee's done surrendered. Place called Appomattox. War's over."

The teamsters cheered. The terrible conflict was finished. The South had lost—but the bloodshed and destruction had come to an end. There would be peace.

Peace! Blunt realization struck Adam Rait forcefully. There was no war. Therefore, there was no point in going to Marshall.

Chapter Nine

In singles, pairs, and small groups the teamsters drifted back into the center of the clearing. Elation was gone; the vine of high-flown dreams and suddenly born ambitions had withered almost before it had thrust forth its first tendril.

Adam Rait considered them in silence, noted also the rapt attention being accorded him by the de Aceras. His head came up abruptly as a thought touched him. The deal with the Confederacy was lost—but there were others.

"Well, mister, reckon this leaves us high and dry."

It was Bill Gannon again, the self-appointed spokesman. The tone of the man's voice rubbed at Adam's nerves but he clung to his temper.

"I'll be drawing what wages I've got coming . . . now."

"Up to you," Adam replied. There was enough money in the roll of currency found on Kurt Hanover to pay off a few of the drivers, if they insisted, but he knew he could not settle in full. "Maybe you won't be wanting it."

"God damn it. Don't try euchring me!" Gannon flared. "War's over. Army ain't got no use for the rifles and cartridges now!"

"There's Mexico."

"Mexico! Juárez!" Joe Denver yelled, suddenly remembering. "That Escobar. He was wanting to buy!"

Rait nodded, lifted his hands to still the hubbub. Looking directly at Gannon, he spoke loudly enough for all to hear.

"You're right. The Confederacy has no need for the cargo now, but I'm not of a mind to turn it over to the Yankees who'll pay us nothing."

Again he had to quiet the men. "But we've got another customer if you're willing to risk your necks. It means crossing Comanche country . . . and there'll be plenty of renegades fresh out of the Army, looking for a stake."

Adam paused, allowed his words to have their effect. He glanced to the de Aceras. Angela and Hernando were now inside the barouche, listening intently. She had one arm resting on the door, her eyes on him.

"I expect there's enough of us to take care of a few renegades and Indians," Rufus Moore drawled. "What're you getting at?"

"Benito Juárez and his revolution," Rait said. "That man who drove up when we were unloading . . . he was a Juárez agent. He wanted to buy the cargo from Hanover."

"Sell to the Mexicans?" Gannon shouted. "Not on your tintype, mister! Wouldn't give them the sweat offen my nose!"

76

"You'd rather give the guns to the Yankees? Throw away a thousand in gold?"

Gannon wagged his head. "Ain't got no use for greasers. Got my belly full of them in 'Forty-Six when I was soldiering down there with Johnny Wool."

"Nobody's asking you to side with them. All you'll have to do is drive your wagon to Juárez City."

Gannon muttered something unintelligible, fingering the whip coiled about his shoulder.

Another teamster pushed forward. "How you know you can trust this here Juárez? I was with Zach Taylor, and I'm stringing along with Bill and what he's saying."

Adam shrugged. "The way I see it, we'll have to trust him, same as we'd have to trust anybody else we made a deal with. I figure we can."

Joe Denver said: "We could set ourselves down on this side of the Río Grande, stand pat until they bring us the gold."

There was a quick shout of approval for the suggestion. Rait lifted his arms.

"What's more, Juárez's agent offered to make a down payment on the cargo. Don't know how much . . . five, maybe ten thousand dollars. If something went wrong, we'd have that much to split."

"Be better'n wages!"

"Dang' right, and a little's better'n nothing a-tall!"

"Well, I sure ain't for giving nothing to the god-damn' Yankees."

"Me, neither. I vote we head for Mexico!"

"All right!" Rait had to shout to make himself heard. "Voting's the way to decide it, but first I aim to get something straight with you."

He paused, again looked squarely at Bill Gannon. "If we make a deal with Juárez, every man who agrees to go . . . goes all the way. There'll be no backing out. That clear?"

"You won't be fretting over me," Lars Larsen declared. "With a thousand in gold I can start me that horse ranch I been wanting."

"Let's put it to a vote, then. Men who are with me, step over to this side of the clearing."

There was a general shift, and when it was over only Bill Gannon and Henry Fox had not moved. At once the other teamsters began to shout and harangue.

Fox waved his arms. "You jaspers don't know what you're voting yourselves into. You got any idea how far it is to Juárez City? Be better'n a month's hard driving. And on them hard tails . . ."

"Fix yourself an extra blanket, Henry."

"And that ain't all. Like Rait said, there'll be a plenty Comanches. Maybe a few Kiowas and Apaches, along with busted-out soldiers on the loose. They'll be mean and hungry, bad as the Comanches, even worse."

"Well, we got ourselves a pretty good little

army right here," Jeremy Haskins, a squat Missourian, said. "And plenty of guns and ammunition . . . was we to need them."

"Reckon we could put us up one hell of a scrap at that," Darby Sims commented.

Adam waited for the talk to fade. When all was quiet, he faced Fox and the scowling Bill Gannon. He needed them both—not only because they were expert teamsters but there would be times *en route* when every gun would count. To believe they could move the train eight hundred miles across the hostile land unmolested was sheer nonsense.

"I've got enough cash to pay you both off . . . but I'd like to have you stick with us. It's going to take one man driving and one standing ready with a rifle on each rig, all the way. How about it?"

Fox gave Gannon a slanting look, shrugged his thick shoulders, and started across the clearing. "Reckon if you birds figure you can make it, I can, too."

Bill Gannon watched the Missourian for a moment, spat, and then, swaggering slightly, followed. Instantly a cheer went up. Adam silenced the men.

"I want to say this once more. You're giving me your word . . . nobody backs out."

"Won't be none of that," someone answered. "Let's get to rolling."

Again the crew turned away, moved hurriedly

for their wagons. Rait caught at Denver, halted him. "Joe, I've got a job for you."

The teamster wheeled. "Something special?"

"Take Hanover's horse and ride back to Galveston."

"Get Escobar, that it?"

Adam nodded. "He said, if we wanted him, he'd be at a friend's place. Francisco Chavez. Probably a *hacienda* at the edge of town."

"What'll I tell him?"

"That we're ready to make a deal. Bring him back with you . . . along with all the cash he can scrape up. We'll be needing supplies."

"You going to wait here?"

"No, we'll pull out right away. I want to get across the Trinity. Expect the best place to meet you'll be on the Brazos."

"It means you'll be cutting due west."

"For the first few days."

"Ought to put you somewheres around Dackett."

"Make it a couple of miles below. I aim to stay clear of towns. The less people know we're traveling through, the smaller chance there is for trouble. Likely we'll be getting there first, so we'll wait."

"I'll find you," Denver said, turning toward Hanover's tall black. "So long."

Adam lifted his hand in salute, his mind already swinging to other matters. He'd put Gannon on the lead wagon. He didn't like the man, trusted him not at all, but there was no avoiding the fact that he was one of the best.

And the de Aceras. That was something else that must be attended to. He called instructions to Gannon, placing him in charge of the teamsters, and crossed to the de Acera carriage.

Hernando stepped out to meet him, polite and stiffly formal. Angela remained inside the barouche, cool and aloof. Adam touched the brim of his hat.

"A decision to change our plans has been made," he said in Spanish.

De Acera bobbed his head. "It was heard . . . because of your war's end. It is understandable."

"We travel west, no longer north to Marshall. I regret we must part here."

"Of course," Hernando said, bowing slightly. "But does not Fort Worth lie to the west, also? Would it be possible to continue our journey in your company to a point below the city of Austin? When there, we could turn north to Fort Worth."

Hernando was correct in his understanding of directions, but Adam was in no mood to shoulder any more responsibility than had already been thrust upon him. It was best to look at the situation from the worst possible viewpoint—that from then on the train would be a prize certain to attract every plunder-hungry renegade and Indian in southern Texas.

"We shall avoid the main roads," he explained.

"You will find greater safety in going on to Marshall."

"As you say," Hernando replied, disappointed but still polite. "It is farewell, then. A thousand thanks for your company."

"It is nothing," Rait said, and glanced up to see Angela studying him thoughtfully. She smiled, and, touching his hat, he turned away.

Chapter Ten

Leaning forward in the barouche, Angela thrust her head outside and said: "Sergeant, stop beneath those trees."

Obediently Martinez swung the carriage off the road and halted it in the shade of several clustering pecans.

Hernando—in reality General Hernando Bernal of His Royal Majesty Maximilian's Imperial Mexican Guards and in no way related to Angela de Acera—kicked open the door and leaped out. Walking quickly to the top of a hillock fifty yards back on the road, he threw his glance to the west. Within moments he returned.

"They cannot see us here," he said, climbing into the carriage.

Angela shrugged. Such had been apparent to her, but Bernal, with his infernal military efficiency, had to make sure. She watched idly as he drew a cigar from his pocket, placed it between his lips, and struck a match. She decided she'd never learn to like the man.

He exhaled a cloud of blue smoke, settled back. "It is necessary to make new plans," he said briskly. "Although we encounter failure, nothing must dissuade us."

Angela brushed at the film of dust gathered on

her lap. Outside, Martinez had moved off his perch and was fiddling with the harness. The day was warming rapidly, and soon the heat would be intense.

When she made no comment, Hernando said: "Haste is now of importance. My soldiers await their instructions."

Angela stirred. "Of what use are twelve soldiers against thirty well-armed men such as accompany Adam Rait?"

"Twenty-seven, if one does not count the cook, the boy, and the hostler. I do not speak of a squad, but of a company awaiting my word at a secret base."

"Just where is this mysterious rendezvous, General?"

"A matter of no importance to you, my lady," Bernal replied with an offhand motion. "At this moment they are valueless to our movements anyway. We were cautioned not to bring uniformed soldiers onto North American soil. The government cannot afford to further antagonize the United States."

"I recall well what was said."

Hernando sighed. "It is a matter I find most difficult to understand. With my own eyes I have seen soldiers of the Indian Juárez on this side of the border. Why is it permissible for them but not . . . ?"

"The North Americans prefer to ignore their

presence. Perhaps it has to do with their own war against the English king a hundred years ago. They believe Benito Juárez to be engaged in a similar struggle."

"The *gringos* and their wars. It was an evil blow that this most recent one has ended. It creates serious complications. Even so, had you not failed to persuade Hanover . . ."

"He was very drunk," Angela cut in coldly. "So much so there was no reasoning with the man."

"Very possibly, yet had you yielded to his desires, a bargain may have later been struck."

"He was very drunk," Angela repeated. "As to the other, my judgment is best."

"Very well. There is nothing that can be done about him since he is dead."

"An error on your part, my General. Had you not acted in panic and ordered Martinez to use his knife, a second opportunity may have been afforded me."

Bernal frowned darkly. "I did so in the best interests of my country. When failure became evident . . ."

"You listened outside the tent?"

"I did, in the nature of duty. When it was evident this Hanover would not succumb to your . . . shall we say charms? . . . I determined such action was necessary. Of this I was convinced when I recalled Hanover's words wherein he said that Adam Rait was his heir should an accident befall him."

"A jest."

Hernando smiled knowingly. "It would seem you assume in error. Has not the wagon train with its cargo become the property of Rait?"

"Of him . . . and those who accompany him."

The officer shifted irritably. "Another matter I cannot comprehend. What sort of man is this Adam Rait who gives away a fortune that rightfully becomes his?"

Angela considered Hernando Bernal through half-closed eyelids and wished again that those in command at Mexico City had selected a different officer to accompany her on the mission. But there had been reason for it, and while it was not pleasant, she would make the best of a disagreeable situation.

But she didn't have to like the man. He was a small-minded puppet, given to show and the display of unnecessary authority. Callous, ruthless, and weighted with the supercilious snobbery of the elite military, he still was not above groveling and self-abasement if by them his purpose could be achieved.

"No, he is one you will never understand," she murmured, staring out across the flats.

"Eh? Oh . . . it is of no importance. Let us think, my lady. Let us put our heads together and devise a plan of infallibility."

Bernal tossed his cigar through the window. Leaning forward, he placed his hand on Angela's knee and pressed gently. "But that your efforts with Hanover should not go unrewarded, I . . ."

She brushed his fingers away. "The general forgets himself."

Bernal frowned. "I do not understand!"

"I believe you do," she replied coldly. "I accompany you for the sake of Mexico . . . and Maximilian. I shall do the job I was assigned . . . that of convincing Kurt Hanover, by any means in my power, to . . ."

"A dead man cannot be convinced of anything."

"Very well. I must try to convince Adam Rait to sell to us the cargo of rifles and bullets in his possession. Beyond that I have no obligation . . . particularly to you."

The general shrugged. "Let us not quarrel."

"Let us not indulge in wayward thoughts," Angela snapped. "As you have said, we are faced with change. Do you have a plan?"

Bernal, still sulky, drew forth another cigar, held it poised. "I have. One of simplicity."

Simplicity. That, of course, meant the persuasion of Adam Rait would depend upon her. Angela looked at Hernando and waited.

"We follow the wagon train at a discreet distance. Since it moves generally westward, it is to our advantage. Escobar has been sent for. Martinez will be dispatched to prevent his arrival, thus voiding the intended agreement before it can be made."

The officer paused, studied the unlit end of his weed. "At the proper time we will make a reappearance. Our position will be made known, and your ties will begin. Meanwhile, Martinez will continue to the secret base along the border and advise the troops to hold themselves in readiness."

"You will make use of these soldiers?"

"Should you again fail," Bernal said, spacing his words deliberately, "I shall abandon the plan thought to be effective by those in the court, and resort to the more dependable military. I will breach North American soil and take the wagon train by force."

Angela, ignoring the sly jibe, nodded. "A sensible plan, although you risk displeasure of both governments. Is this base where your soldiers wait near the border?"

"Very near," he said. "I have hopes their use will not be necessary. You have doubts as to your effectiveness with this Adam Rait?"

She smiled. "Who knows? There is an old saying among the North Americans, my General. One never counts chickens before they are hatched. It is a wise proverb."

Hernando Bernal frowned. "But if one hesitates to try," he began, missing the point entirely, "I fail to see . . ."

"It is of little consequence," Angela said wearily. "Can we now move? The heat is unbearable."

"Agreed." The officer turned to the window. "Sergeant!"

Martinez, dozing in the shade thrown by the horses, scrambled to his feet, hurried to the side of the carriage.

"Yes, my General!"

"Return to the settlement near to where we encountered the North American, Hanover. We will rid ourselves of this accursed hearse and obtain saddle horses and clothing more befitting our duties in the days to come. Make haste!"

Chapter Eleven

Late in the afternoon of the second day Adam Rait, astride the bay gelding, watched as the wagons, one by one, and with spare teams standing by ready for emergency use, forded the Brazos River. The crossing was made without incident, and he swung the train south, pointing for a distant grove of trees that would serve as an acceptable location for night camp.

There was no sign of Denver and Emiliano Escobar, and that disturbed him somewhat. The train, delayed by slow progress due to the loose nature of the soil over which they traveled, was several hours late, and he had expected the men to be there well ahead of the column. That they were not could only mean Denver, too, had encountered trouble in some form. Perhaps he was having difficulty in locating Escobar. And there was the possibility the Mexican agent had returned to Juárez City.

Adam considered that at length, concluded it would not seriously affect his plan for selling the cargo to Benito Juárez and his government. Failing to negotiate a prearranged deal with Escobar along with a request for an escort that surely would be needed, he would simply have to proceed without either.

Juárez would buy the rifles and ammunition—there was no doubt as to that—but it would take more time. He would follow Joe Denver's suggestion of setting up camp on the American side of the border and riding on to Juárez City to talk with the Mexican *presidente* himself. When all was agreed upon and payment in gold was available, delivery would be completed.

The wagons reached the grove and swung into their customary formation. By the time the teamsters had seen to their equipment and Adam had made his usual inspection, Felipe was rattling the bucket, summoning all to the evening meal. Ordinarily garrulous, the men were quiet, eating their food and drinking their bitter coffee with only occasional comments. It had been a hard day.

When supper was over, and the teamsters had begun to unroll their blankets, Adam called Felipe to him. He felt a fire should be maintained throughout the night as a guide for Denver and Escobar, should they have trouble locating the camp. Not a big one, he explained to the boy; he didn't want to attract the curious from nearby Dackett, but a small, steady blaze that could be spotted by someone moving along the river.

When Felipe signified his understanding and hurried off to drag in a supply of dry wood, Rait turned to Sancho. "They'll be hungry. Have food ready." The cook nodded and immediately began to fill two plates from his blackened pots.

Adam, restless, drew one of the cigars removed from Hanover's effects from his pocket and returned to the fire for a light.

Jules Bundy, sitting nearby sucking at his pipe, looked up. "Suppose something's happened to Joe?"

Adam shook his head. "He'll be here."

The teamster puffed thoughtfully. "Yeah, reckon he will."

Rait wheeled slowly, strolled to a low hump a short distance below the camp. The night was warm with only a suggestion of a breeze filtering in from the south, carrying with it the pleasant promise of spring. Overhead the sky was dark velvet across which diamond dust had been flung.

Finding a stump, Adam sat down, inhaled deeply, and allowed the smoke to trickle from his mouth. He could hear Sancho rattling pans as he finished up his work, and Felipe was throwing more wood onto the fire, building the blaze. One of the men—he had no idea who—was singing an old Southern favorite, "Lorena", in a surprisingly good tenor voice.

He listened until the sorrowing words ended and found himself thinking of Angela de Acera, remembering the way she looked that night they had walked in the grove.

She was a woman to move a man deeply, turn him from his purpose, and hold him tight in a snare of excitement. He was glad he had insisted she and her brother continue on to Marshall. Having her near, seeing her, feeling her soft eyes upon him, was a disturbing influence—and he could afford no distractions.

But she was not so easily forgotten, and he found it difficult to wipe her from his mind. He inhaled again, enjoying the bite of smoke in his lungs. Maybe—when this was all over and he had money in his pockets—he'd take a ride up to Fort Worth and see if he could find her. . . .

A halloo from across the river brought him to his feet. Joe Denver. At last! Tossing aside the cigar, he trotted back to camp. Shortly Denver, followed by Emiliano Escobar, rode out of the darkness into the circle of firelight.

Both men were worn, covered with dust. A bloodstained bandage was wrapped around the Mexican's right arm. They dismounted stiffly, turned their horses over to the wrangler.

"We would've been here a couple hours sooner," Denver said, looking toward the chuck wagon, "only some pot-licker tried to ambush us. The *señor* got nicked."

Escobar smiled. "It is of no consequence." He accepted the plate of food Sancho offered him, thanking the old cook in his quiet, grave manner.

"Any idea who it was?" Rait asked as the men began to eat. Several of the teamsters, aroused by the arrival, had moved up to the fire.

Joe swallowed a large mouthful. "Road agent looking for easy pickings, I expect. Give him something to be remembering. Winged him when he took off."

It came as a surprise to no one. The country was overrun with hungry men, broke and desperate, looking to make a dollar in any way possible.

Escobar finished his meal quickly, consuming about half the portion Sancho had put on his plate. Handing the dish to the cook, he thanked him again, faced Adam. "My heart was gladdened by the words brought to me by *Señor* Denver. The people of Mexico will forever be in your debt."

"Matter of business," Rait replied. "We're selling and you're buying. You in position to make a deal?"

"I am. The value of the cargo, as I recall, was placed at forty thousand dollars in gold. Is that not correct?"

"It is. It was Hanover's figure, however, not mine."

"He was an honest man and I have no reason to dispute the amount. It is agreeable, and I am empowered by my government to negotiate on that basis. Payment is to be made upon delivery to Juárez City."

"Agreed. You mentioned a token payment . . . to bind the contract."

Escobar frowned. "To be sure. However, there

was not sufficient time to obtain any large amount. I have with me slightly more than two thousand dollars."

One of the teamsters swore in disappointment. Adam was silent; he had hoped for more— much more. Not that he mistrusted the Juárez government, but a long trip lay ahead of them and there would be need for expense money. He had also entertained the idea of advancing wages to the crew; cash jingling in a man's pockets was always a strong morale builder.

Finally he said: "It'll have to do."

Escobar, relieved, removed a money belt from around his waist and handed it to Rait. "You will find gold in the amount of two thousand one hundred forty . . ."

"Make it an even two thousand," Adam cut in. "It'll be easier to keep up with round figures."

Escobar said—"As you wish."—and, opening the belt, removed the odd amount.

Adam accepted the leather container and hung it over his shoulder. "I've been thinking about an armed escort. I figure we'll need it, once we reach the border. You should ride on ahead."

"Such is my intent. Do you know the village of Tupelo? It is what you call in your language a crossroads."

"Been there once."

"I shall arrange for the escort to meet you there. To that end I leave at once."

"No need for that much hurry. Morning will be soon enough."

"I am accustomed to little sleep. Also I am anxious to notify President Juárez. If it is possible to exchange my tired horse . . . ?"

"Sure," Rait said, motioning to the wrangler. "Polo, pick out a good mount from the remuda."

The hostler rose and hurried off into the night. Escobar glanced at Sancho and Rait suggested: "Perhaps a little food for him to carry."

The cook hustled toward the chuck wagon. Emiliano Escobar brought his attention back to Rait. "Will you cross the border before you reach Tupelo?"

"Not until we meet the escort. It'll be safer on this side."

"There is little safety on either side, I fear," the Juárista said. "I will hasten the soldiers. Perhaps it will be possible to meet you at an earlier date."

"Be obliged."

Polo returned leading a fresh horse wearing Escobar's ornate Mexican gear. Sancho appeared, carrying a flour sack a quarter filled with food and tied it onto the saddle horn. Escobar mounted at once and settled himself.

"There is one matter of caution I must impress upon you. Do not confuse the soldiers of the Royalists with those of the Republic. A large force of the Austrian usurper hides along the border where it preys upon our supply trains and patrols. They wear blue uniforms with much gold braid in evidence."

Adam extended his hand. "We'll know the difference. *Adiós, señor.*"

Escobar smiled. "*Adiós. Buena suerte.*"

When the agent had disappeared into the shadows, Rait turned to the men. "You heard," he said. "Deal's all set . . . and we've got two thousand in gold as a starter. I figure to spread it around . . ." A cheer interrupted him. He waited a few moments, continued. "Won't be much. Taking on this long a haul calls for more supplies. I'll stock up at the next town. What's left we'll divide."

Again there were yells of approval. Old Malachi Lee rubbed at his mouth. "Could sure use me some drinking liquor. What's the next town, and when'll we be getting there?"

"Jonesburg," Adam said. "Ought to reach it about dark, day after tomorrow."

Lee clawed at his beard happily. "Well, how-de-do. I sure am going to get me rolling drunk."

"Don't bank on it," Bill Gannon said sourly. "I'm betting we don't never see any of that gold."

Chapter Twelve

Jonesburg was seventeen dilapidated houses, one livery stable, three saloons, a general store, and a half a dozen deserted, hollow-eyed buildings. Adam Rait, an hour or so in advance of the wagon train, pulled up to the sagging hitch rack fronting the mercantile establishment and halted.

An aura of decay clung to the settlement, and while far removed from the theater of war and therefore unscarred by fire and cannon, it lay dying, nevertheless. Isolated and ignored, long-range strangulation had long since set it, and those souls trapped within its confines, powerless to escape, now existed in a sort of parasitical vacuum.

There was no one on the rotting boardwalks of the street. On the porch of each saloon several men lounged, watching Rait narrowly as he dismounted, climbed the two steps to the store, and entered.

The interior of the building was stifling, loaded with stale, trapped air. Flies buzzed noisily about a molasses keg in a far corner, and the shelving on the walls was half empty.

No one appeared and Adam crossed to a counter and rapped sharply on the splintered wood.

Moments later an elderly man came from behind a curtained doorway in the rear. He placed both hands, palms down, on the counter, surveyed Rait with flat eyes.

"Yeah?"

"Here to buy supplies," Adam said.

"What kind of money you got?" the storekeeper asked without changing expression. Evidently news of the Confederacy's collapse had reached Jonesburg."

"Gold."

The storekeeper relented, and he became almost friendly. "What'll you be needing?"

Adam ran his glance along the dusty shelves. "Lots more than I can see here. There another town close?"

The old man wagged his head. "Dackett . . . east of here. Next stop west'll be more'n a hundred mile. Things are hard to get. Been a war going on."

"I know," Rait answered dryly. Taking a folded slip of paper from his pocket, he passed it to the storekeeper. "Do the best you can with that list."

"Powerful lot of eatables," the man said, slowly checking the items. "You bringing a wagon train or something through here?"

A slyness had crept into the storekeeper's manner. Adam said: "Or something. How soon will you have my order ready?"

"Couple hours."

Rait nodded. "Put it in boxes," he said, and turned for the door.

Several of the saloon bums had bestirred themselves and now loafed on the porch of the store. They pulled back lazily, allowed Rait to pass between them. No one spoke, but that they had overheard all that was said inside was evident. He stepped down into the ankle-deep dust, halted, eyes on the largest of the saloons.

A wariness had grown within him, and he was having second thoughts about turning the crew loose in Jonesburg. With so many idle men hanging around there was more than a good chance for trouble, and while he had no doubt the hard-edged teamsters could take care of themselves, he wanted no undue attention drawn to the train—and there was always the possibility of loose talk.

But Malachi Lee had expressed the needs of all the men. Teamsters were a special breed, and whiskey was as essential to their well-being as the food they ate.

He crossed to the saloon, doing some rapid calculating on the way, and roused the man dozing behind the bar.

"Need ten gallons of good whiskey. Got a keg you can put it in?"

The bartender stared at him as though uncertain of his hearing. "You say ten gallons?"

Rait nodded. "Don't want any of your red-eye. I want the best you stock."

The saloon man was suddenly galvanized into action. He hadn't made a sale like this in years. "Yes, sir, got some of Beam's best. Bourbon. Been hanging onto it . . . sort of saving it for special doings. That be all right?"

"How much?" Adam said.

The man considered. Finally: "Reckon I'll have to get about seventy-five dollars for that much. Good liquor ain't cheap."

Rait drew forth his money sack, counted out the stipulated amount. "Be back for it in a little while," he said, and left the building.

He had planned to rejoin the train when his purchasing was finished and send Felipe with the light wagon to pick up the supplies. He was having doubts as to the wisdom of that, also. He could avoid that problem if he handled the matter himself, but that would require his going back for the light wagon.

With the additional supplies an extra vehicle wouldn't be such a bad idea he decided, and, making up his mind, he recrossed the street to Erdman's Livery Barn. Here again he had difficulty in rousing the owner. When the man eventually materialized from the gloomy shadows in the rear, Adam made his wants known: a light wagon, canvas top if possible, and a team to pull it.

"Got four second-hand wagons out back," Erdman said. "Make the price right."

Adam nodded. "Horses?"

"Might skeerce. Show you what I got."

Typical of horse dealers, Erdman made no further comment, simply led Rait to a corral on the north side of the barn and waited for his reaction.

There were a dozen or so animals in the enclosure, none of them particularly noteworthy. There were far better horses loafing in the remuda, Rait knew, but they were miles away with the train and being intentionally led around the town by Joe Denver.

Adam spent a half hour in the corral, selecting what he felt to be the best two animals in the lot. Erdman helped him herd them into an adjoining pen.

"How much?" Rait asked when that was done.

Erdman stroked his chin. "You got yourself prime stock there, mister. You're a good judge of fine horseflesh. Have to have a hundred apiece."

"I'm a better judge than that," Adam snapped. "I'll go a hundred for the pair."

The stable owner groaned. "God dammit, man. That's plain stealing!"

"Neither one of those broomtails is worth more'n twenty-five dollars . . . and you know it. Wouldn't offer that if I had time to scout around." Rait paused, drew out his money pouch, and produced several coins. "I pay off in gold, Erdman. Make up your mind."

"I'll take it," the man said quickly. "You'll be wanting a bill of sale."

Adam nodded. "And harness . . . and one of those spring wagons. One with the red wheels will do. How much?"

"Make it a hundred and fifty for the lot."

Rait counted out the money. "Show me the harness, and I'll be hitching up while you make out the papers."

Another hour had passed before he had collected his load. With the bay tied to the tailgate of the new wagon and his pistol prominently displayed in his lap, he rolled out of Jonesburg under the eyes of the townspeople.

Mindful of their attention, he headed due south for the first two miles, and then, well beyond sight of the settlement, cut west. He wasn't certain why he took such precautions, but somehow it seemed like a good idea.

He caught up with the train about dark, and turning the wagon over to one of the extra drivers, mounted the bay and led the cavalcade into a small grove not far from a small river where they halted for the night.

There was some grumbling when he announced the town was to be avoided, but that dissatisfaction faded quickly when he had the keg of

whiskey rolled out and placed on the open tailgate of the supply wagon.

There was a noisy clamor for cups, and then
Adam felt a hand on his arm.

Joe Denver said: "We got us some company."

Rait followed the direction of the teamster's
gaze. Facing them in a semicircle were a half a
hundred soldiers. All were dressed in Confederate
gray.

Chapter Thirteen

Alert, a strong current of suspicion filtering through him, Adam Rait moved slowly from the rear of the wagon to the center of the camp. Silent, the teamsters began to fan out to either side. Bill Gannon, muttering under his breath, hitched at his pistol belt. Adam stayed him with a lifted hand.

The leader of the soldiers, a lean, hollow-cheeked man with deep-set, glowing eyes, a full beard, and down-curving mustache, spurred his horse forward. A saber hung at his side, and a revolver was thrust into the red sash encircling his waist. He wore the three gold stars of a colonel on his tattered coat that bore the yellow facing of the cavalry. A feathery plume had been stuck into the band of his wilted brim hat, reflecting evident admiration for Confederate General Beauty Stuart or perhaps the Partisan Ranger, John Mosby.

He halted a dozen paces in front of Rait. Immediately the young lieutenant who had remained a horse length behind him motioned to a thick-shouldered sergeant to stand fast, also advanced.

"Kurt Hanover?"

The senior officer's speech was affected by

that usual shibboleth of the South wherein there seemed to be a dearth of r's in the alphabet. Thus, the blockade runner's name came out something like Kuht Hanovah.

"Hanover's dead," Adam said.

Surprise and annoyance crossed the Confederate's features. It was as though he considered the man's demise a gross personal affront.

"Who're you, mister?"

"Adam Rait."

"This is Hanover's wagon train."

It was a statement rather than a question. Adam allowed his gaze to slide over the line of ragged cavalrymen. Some held pistols, others rifles or old, muzzleloading muskets. A few sabers were in view, and the entire company acted as though they were unaware of the war's end.

"It was."

The officer nodded in satisfaction. "Permit me to introduce myself, sir. Colonel Zebulon Cook of the Third Missouri Cavalry . . . Confederate."

One of the teamsters, Earl Handy, laughed. "Hell, soldier boy, go on home. Fighting's over."

Zebulon Cook's eyes blazed with sudden fire. He made an imperious gesture with a gauntleted hand, barked: "Lieutenant Griswold, I want that man arrested!"

The junior officer goaded his horse forward, then halted. "He's a civilian, sir."

"Civilian or not . . . arrest him!"

Bill Gannon settled back on his heels. His bullet head dropped slightly. Abruptly the moment was charged with the promise of violence. Adam took another step toward Cook, breaking the tension.

"You're not arresting anybody, Colonel."

At Rait's cool declaration the officer crossed his hands on the saddle horn, rested his weight on his arms. "You aware this area's under military control?"

"Not likely. The war's ended. Lee surrendered a couple of weeks ago. Must be something wrong with your communications."

"Lee surrendered, we didn't!" Cook shouted, stiffening. "The Army of the South is still fighting. It will continue to fight . . . down to the last man!"

"What army?" Rait asked quietly.

"The true Confederate Army! Mine . . . and General Kirby Smith, camped at Shreveport . . . Shelby . . . and many others. We plan to unite . . . fight on!"

"Crazy as a peach-orchard boar," Joe Denver murmured under his breath.

"War's a long way from being over, mister. And don't you forget it," Cook continued, his voice rising steadily. "Lee quit, but not us! We'll *never* quit!"

Adam shrugged. "You're fooling yourself, Colonel. It's finished. The South lost. Face it."

"You in the Army?" Cook broke in.

"Three years. Same Missouri Cavalry you're talking about. I was with Dixon."

"Ah, yes, Dixon. Fine officer. Lost in a skirmish near Memphis."

Got me a little souvenir there, too, right in the leg, Adam thought, but he said nothing.

Cook was staring at him, impaling him with a baleful glare. "You desert?"

"Discharged. Medical."

"No man gets discharged from the Army of the Confederacy!" the officer shouted. "I order you to report to me at . . ."

"What do you want, Colonel?" Rait demanded, impatience finally getting the best of him.

"Want? You have the gall to ask me that? You a thief . . . a deserter?"

"I'm asking."

"I want the ordnance Hanover contracted to supply and that you have diverted to your own purpose!"

The missing parts of the picture fell into place for Adam. Kurt's deal had been with the Confederate Army, so much he knew, but with whom exactly had never been clear. Evidently Cook had been involved, as perhaps were Shelby and Kirby Smith.

He wondered if those two officers were actually with Cook, as he had implied, in his mad plan to continue the war, but Rait decided it was unlikely. It was more logical to assume the colonel was endeavoring to raise and equip a force of his own, and, being aware of the contract with Kurt Hanover, had seized upon it as a means for accomplishing his aims.

Cook's shrill voice broke into his thoughts. "I demand to know by what right you have diverted this ordnance from its intended destination?"

"The war ended. The Confederacy has no need for it."

"I repeat, I do not recognize the surrender at Appomattox! The loyal men of the Confederate Army will continue to fight the northern invaders!"

"I doubt that. The war was lost a long time ago. Most Southerners realized that, only the leaders wouldn't face up. . . ."

"Treason!" Zebulon Cook shrieked, darkening with anger. "I'll have you before a firing squad for those words!"

"You keep yammering like that and you'll get yourself a battle right here!" Gannon shouted, pushing by Rait. "Was fools like you that got a lot of good men killed for nothing."

"Arrest him!" Cook cried. "Instantly!"

Lieutenant Griswold spurred ahead. Immediately there was a stirring among the teamsters. Adam moved quickly, seized the bridle of the officer's horse.

"Another fool stunt like that and somebody'll blow your head off," he warned.

Gannon once more crowded to the fore. "Let him try arresting me. Just let him try."

Again the moment was a powder keg, awaiting the slightest spark to turn the clearing into a wholesale bloodletting.

The lieutenant returned Adam's fixed gaze. "Let go my horse, mister."

"When you start backing up. Take a good look around. Probably two dozen guns pointing at your belly."

"You look behind me," Griswold said. "You'll see fifty leveled at you."

"No doubt. But you keep thinking that you'll be the first to go down if somebody makes a wrong move."

The young officer hesitated, swallowed hard.

"Lieutenant Griswold. What's the delay there?" Cook's voice echoed strangely through the trees.

Adam released his grip on the bridle, faced the senior officer.

"The deal you're talking about's off, Colonel," he said, giving Griswold opportunity to back down gracefully while he held Cook's attention. "When we got word of the surrender, we made other plans. The cargo's sold to somebody else now."

Volatile one instant, Zebulon Cook could be equally calm the next. "You had no right to make such a decision. No authority. The Army of the

Confederacy needs those rifles . . . must in fact have them in order to carry on. Are you aware, mister, that I am empowered to confiscate the goods . . . and pay you nothing?"

"I'm aware that you can't . . . legally." Adam Rait was also calm, although only by great effort. He shifted his attention to the line of silent soldiers. "What the hell's the matter with you men? Get it straight in your head. The war's over. There's no more Confederacy. You think you can fight a private war of your own against the whole United States Army?"

There was no response from the ragged gray scarecrows. Adam wiped at the sweat gathered on his forehead.

"You can't win, no matter what you've been told. Best thing you can do is pull out. Go home."

The sergeant behind Cook transferred his weight from the right to left stirrup. "Reckon we'll stick with the colonel," he said in a rich drawl.

"Why? If a man's going to die, it ought to be for something."

"The colonel knows what he's a doing."

"That'll do, Sergeant!" Cook snapped. "I need no defense from these . . . these traitorous . . ."

"You're sure needing something," Malachi Lee called from his place among the teamsters. "I 'spect it might be brains."

A laugh went up, but only from Malachi's

fellow drivers. Another voice shouted: "Gen'ral, you got forty thousand in gold on you? That's what this here cargo'll cost you."

"Hell's a-frying, Zeke! The Confederacy ain't never seen forty thousand dollars in gold!"

"You'll be given an order from the Treasury of the Confederate States," Cook said, breaking in quietly. "Upon proper presentation you will receive payment in whatever form you wish. Such was the agreement."

"Agreement was cash on delivery . . . in gold," Rait said. "If you can meet those terms, we can do business."

There was no likelihood of that, Adam knew, and he was not endangering his promise to Emiliano Escobar and the Juárez government. He was simply searching for a way to bring the confrontation to a close; there were far too many nervous trigger fingers gathered in the clearing.

"You will receive an order," Zebulon Cook repeated patiently. "If such isn't satisfactory, I will be compelled to confiscate the goods in the name of the Confederate Army."

"Like hell you will!" Bill Gannon yelled, and jerked out his pistol.

The night rocked with the sound of gunfire as a half a dozen rifles crashed. Will Gordon, immediately behind Gannon, staggered and fell. The teamsters opened up, the sharper crack of their pistols mingling with the more thunderous report of the long guns. Adam saw two soldiers buckle and tumble from their saddles. Another teamster went down. And a third.

Then he had a glimpse of Zeb Cook, saber waving above his plumed hat, mouth blared wide in a wild, ringing yell, charging down upon him.

Adam tried to save himself, jerk clear of the oncoming horse. He stumbled against the prostrate Gordon, recovered his balance, and whirled, his own pistol coming up quick. The flat of Cook's blade struck him on the side of the head. Lights popped before his eyes and he felt himself going down. . . .

Chapter Fourteen

Stunned, Adam fought to keep from falling under the hoofs of Cook's horse. Confusion swirled around him. He could hear Joe Denver yelling hoarsely, his deep tones overriding the high, cracked voice of Zebulon Cook. Numbly he realized both were close by. There were no more gunshots. He was conscious enough to feel relief.

"Try that again, Colonel . . . and I'll blow your god-damn' guts all over the place!" Denver's savage words drilled into Rait's clearing mind.

"I'll take no such talk from you, or any man!" Cook was still screaming.

"Up to you. If you'd had a lick of sense, you'd've seen this coming and tried to stop it, like he did."

Adam shook his head to dispel the last of the cobwebs. He pulled himself upright. Denver, pistol in hand, was behind him. To his left Cook, still in the saddle, was poised with upraised saber. Soldiers surrounded the clearing where three teamsters lay dead.

"You're under arrest!" Cook shouted his words at Rait. "You and every damned traitor . . ."

"Arrested for what?" Adam snarled, anger driving him hard. He had endeavored to reason with the officer, and the result had been only death for three men, injuries for others.

"Thievery! Theft of property rightfully belonging to the Confederate States of America. For interfering with the prosecution of the war. Treason! You need more reasons?"

"I need one that makes sense," Rait shot back. "You're no different from outlaws, hijackers."

"Wrong! Confiscation, that's the correct term," Cook said, sheathing his blade. Turning his head, he shouted: "Lieutenant Griswold!"

The young officer broke from the ranks, cantered across the clearing. Halting, he saluted smartly. "Yes, sir!"

"Detail ten men to guard these wagons. I don't trust those civilians in Jonesburg any more than I do these."

"Yes, sir. Neither do I, sir."

"Then get these men disarmed and march them into town. They're all under arrest, awaiting trial."

"Yes, sir," Griswold said again, and saluted once more. Then: "What'll I do with them in town?"

"How the devil would I know? Put them in that vacant livery stable, throw a guard around it."

"Yes, sir. What about the dead?"

"What's the count?"

"Four enlisted men. Three teamsters."

"Have Sergeant Slade form a burial detail and attend to them."

"Yes, sir. Uh . . . I was wondering . . ."

"Well, don't wonder about it, mister! Just hop to it! I want to pull out for Marshall before noon tomorrow with those wagons." Abruptly Cook whirled away, his red sash a garish streak in the dim light.

Griswold beckoned to a rifleman standing nearby. "Corporal, take a dozen men, disarm the prisoners. If anybody objects, shoot him."

The non-com threw a half-hearted salute, motioned to the soldiers behind him. "You heard the lieutenant. Let's get at it."

Cook's men began to move among the teamsters. A muttering arose, and Adam Rait recognized again the proximity of danger—and a clash in which the wagon crew could only emerge the heavy loser. Head throbbing from the blow he had taken at the hands of Zeb Cook, he hoisted himself onto a wheel hub where he could be seen by all. But before he could sound his caution, Ed Vernon's voice reached him above the grumbling.

"Cap'n, this what you want us to do . . . hand over our shooting irons?"

"Do what they tell you," Adam answered, relieved.

The murmuring ceased. The elderly corporal looked at Rait and said: "Obliged. No use getting shot up if you don't have to."

"Ain't no use of any of it," Denver barked. "And if you keep listening to that jackass of a colonel, you'll all end up dead."

The non-com smiled. "Sure thing. Now, I'll be taking that whip you got there, too."

Joe Denver swore deeply, allowed the lash coiled around his left shoulder to fall to the ground. Adam handed his belt and pistol to a young private who looked as though he had yet to weather his first shave, and turned to watch the disarming of his men.

All appeared to be going in an orderly fashion. Off to the left he could hear the burial detail at work, using tools removed from the freight wagons. From the edge of the clearing, Zebulon Cook, his aquiline face in shadow, surveyed it all like some remote god.

"Where'll we put these weapons, Corporal?" the young private asked. "Sure could use me one of these here handguns."

"The colonel'll tend to passing them out later," the non-com replied. "Right now be stacking them in that spring wagon over there."

"Who was it that got killed?" Rait asked, turning to Denver.

"Gordon. Was standing close to Bill Gannon. Got the bullet aimed for him. And they shot Ike Williams and George Shaw."

"Many wounded?"

"Few nicks. Nothing serious, I don't think. I'd say the colonel's jackleg cavalry got the worst of the deal. What're you aiming to do? Just don't seem we ought to take this laying down."

"No choice. He's got us by the short hairs . . . but it's a long time till daylight."

Rait felt the muzzle of a rifle dig into his spine. A voice with an unmistakable Georgia accent said: "You all get over there with them others."

The teamsters were being herded into a group on the far side of the clearing. Half of Cook's men were on foot, weapons drawn; the remainder had mounted, were looking on, also with ready weapons. Everything had become strictly military.

"Column, by fours!" Cook bawled.

The soldiers prodded and pushed the wagon men into a four-abreast formation. Cook rode out front, wheeled, faced his prisoners.

"You men," he shouted, "are being taken to Jonesburg where I will try you in a military court! I'll be sitting on the board with three of my officers."

That should insure a unanimous decision on all questions, Adam thought.

"I'll offer you an honorable way out now . . . and not again," Cook went on. "Enlist and become a member of the Confederate States Army. Charges against you will then be dropped."

There was a long moment of silence. It ended when a voice from the ranks of the teamsters said: "I'd as leave go to bed with a rattlesnake as side in with you bushwhacking bastards!"

Cook stiffened. In the flickering light of the fire his face seemed to darken, become almost black, while his eyes fairly popped from his head.

"Sergeant Slade! I want the man who said that."

The non-com with the thick shoulders hurried to the head of the column, began to move along the length.

"Who done that talking? Hear me? Speak up."

There was no response. Reaching the end of the line, Slade retraced his steps, demanding, threatening. Again his only reply was silence and sly grins. Halting before his colonel, he saluted.

"Ain't nobody willing to own up, sir."

"March 'em out!" Cook shouted, verging on apoplexy. "I'll get further into this incident at the trial. By God I will!"

Headed, flanked, and tailed by cavalrymen, Rait and the teamsters were double-timed to Jonesburg. Reaching the end of the street, they were slowed to ordinary pace, and with Zebulon Cook, in solitary grandeur, leading the column in the best captor–captive style, were paraded the full extent of the settlement.

They halted at a sprawling structure at the extreme north end. All had been in darkness when they arrived. Now, as if by magic, lights were appearing in windows everywhere. Jeremy Haskins, standing to Rait's left, grinned through the dust.

"First town I ever woke up without firing a shot," he said. "Just don't feel natural."

As Zeb Cook drew off aloofly to one side of the

119

street, Lieutenant Adrian Griswold, leaving the prisoners in charge of First Sergeant Slade, made a slow circuit of the abandoned livery barn. The building appeared tight.

"Sergeant," he said sharply, coming back into the street. "I want a man at the back and front doors of this place. Also one on each side . . . where the windows are. See to it."

The non-com saluted, spun his horse about, and bellowed a string of names. Griswold waited until the sentries had surrendered their animals to the horse holders and taken up their posts, and then ordered the entrance flung open.

"Forward, march!" he shouted, and moved aside to let the prisoners proceed into the cavernous structure.

"Mister Griswold!"

Griswold quailed slightly at Zebulon Cook's summons. *Now what the hell's wrong?* he wondered, putting spurs to his mount and galloping the short distance to where his colonel sat in kingly majesty. He saluted crisply.

"Yes, sir!"

"Just wondering, Lieutenant, did you inspect the interior of that building for possible weapons and tools that might be employed in an escape before you consigned your prisoners to it?"

Griswold felt the sweat gathering on his neck and face. *The old bastard knows damned well I didn't,* he thought. *Sat there on his fat ass and watched me.* He had a fleeting wish that things could be the way they were before the war—the family plantation in Louisiana; the easy living; the days when you used your quirt on men like Zeb Cook if they stepped in front of you on the street, but that was gone—long gone. . . .

"Well, Lieutenant, did you?"

"No, sir."

"Then I suggest you take a detail and do so at once. Thoroughly, mister!"

"Yes, sir," the young officer said, saluting again. He started to wheel, wishing in that moment that he had not been fool enough to sign up with Zebulon Cook. But the picture had been a glowing one, the promises broad. Maybe there *could* be another plantation. . . .

"And, Lieutenant!"

Now what . . . ? "Yes, sir."

"You'll be a long time making the next grade unless you start using your head for something besides a rack for your hat."

Yes, sir. Go to hell, sir. And I'm not so god-damn' sure I want the next rank, Adrian Griswold thought, but he once more snapped his salute and said—"Yes, sir. Thank you, sir."—and rode on to attend to his duties.

Chapter Fifteen

From the dark safety of a thicket dominated by towering sycamores, Angela and Bernal watched the capture of Adam Rait and his teamsters.

The general shook his head in frustration and anger. "Nothing goes right. Now this Yankee Army takes possession. It would seem our mission is doomed from the beginning."

Angela, dressed in boots, split riding skirt, dark-colored shirt, and wide-brimmed hat, and listening to one of the Yankee officers shouting commands, scarcely heard Bernal. She had watched Adam Rait go down before the charge of the one with the saber, waited breathless until he rose again. When it was apparent that he was not badly hurt, she felt a sense of relief.

She should have no such emotion, she told herself, and firmly turned her thoughts to the problem at hand.

"They leave the wagons," she said. "A pity your soldiers are not near."

Offended, Hernando shrugged. "If it were possible to foresee all . . ."

"An observation only, my General."

The prisoners were being lined up into a column. She moved on a few steps, endeavoring to locate Rait. The men were all on the opposite side of the fire and the intervening glare was somewhat blinding. Finally she saw him, standing near the center.

Adam Rait seemed docile enough, and that was surprising, completely out of character for him. He would not be giving up so easily. No doubt he had something in mind. Although she had but a brief acquaintance with him, she recognized him as one of strong will and not likely to be turned aside without considerable effort.

The column was ready to march, but there was a delay for one reason or another. The officer in command was addressing the prisoners; just what he was saying Angela could not hear. The interlude ended shortly and the teamsters and all of the soldiers, with the exception of those left to guard the wagons, moved out.

"This will be difficult to explain," Bernal said morosely. "I have no liking for the welcome that will await us in Mexico City."

"You surrender too quickly," she said, tucking a stray lock of hair back under her hat. "It is not finished."

"Surrender? Not finished?" the officer echoed stupidly. "How can that be? The Confederate Army has taken possession of our rifles and ammunition . . . will convert them to their own use. We are powerless to prevent it."

"It is not the real army, General," she replied

impatiently. "Had you listened closely you would know this. The American war is truly over. These soldiers are but renegades."

"Renegades or not, what is the difference?"

"None, perhaps . . . except they have no right to the cargo we hope to possess, and it is likely that Adam Rait will not yield with so small a struggle."

"I have seen braver men."

"That is my point. A thought was in his mind, an idea. He looks ahead. A fool would have fought and lost. He did not."

Hernando Bernal sighed. "All is not clear."

"It will be to our advantage to assist him, aid him in an escape."

He nodded vaguely. "If we so aid this Adam Rait, he will perhaps feel certain obligations. Is that what you are thinking, my lady?"

It wasn't exactly, but at least she was getting through to him, Angela thought, and that was important.

"Partly. It is certain that our hopes die if the renegade soldiers are permitted to depart with the shipment of arms."

"Agreed. But how can we bring this about?"

Angela moved her slender shoulders beneath their sheath of cool sateen. "Who knows? From here it is not possible to say. We can only follow, search for opportunity."

"Of course. And once they are assisted, it is

unquestionable this Adam Rait will consider negotiating."

"True. But would not a better plan be to assist and permit them to continue on unaware of our presence? You will recall that the man Escobar advised Rait to take the wagon train to the village of Tupelo?"

"Yes, I recall."

"Is that not in the area of your soldiers and their secret hiding place?"

Hernando Bernal's features lighted. "Certainly. What could be more convenient than to lead the wagons into their reach? What luck. Do you know they are called the Ghost Soldiers by the Indians?"

"No, I was not aware."

"They strike swiftly and disappear. Strike again, and vanish. It is said they drive the Juáristas mad."

"A most clever arrangement, my General. Do you favor the plan?"

"It is perfect. However, Adam Rait will not cross the border . . . he has said as much. And I hesitate to ignore my orders from Mexico City and bring my men onto foreign soil. It would be wise for you first to make an effort. . . ."

"That is understood. But it would also be wise to be moving toward the secret rendezvous in event . . ."

"In event you again fail, is that it?"

"There is always the possibility."

Hernando Bernal smiled broadly. "I fear Mexico City overestimates the powers of women in such matters as this. The military . . . the force of arms . . . it does not fail."

"Yes, my General," Angela said, also smiling.

Chapter Sixteen

After Griswold had marched them in, back out, and in again, Adam Rait gathered the teamsters in the center of the barn where the intersecting runways formed a large square.

"Got to move fast and quiet," he said. "Handy, you stay at the front doors. Cushman, take the back. Sing out if you see anybody coming."

"What're you aiming to do, Cap'n?" Vernon asked.

"Find a way out of here."

"Ain't going to be easy. That lieutenant and his bunch went through here good."

"That lieutenant's not up against what we are."

"We might get a chance to make a break in the morning," Jim Gooch said. "Was we to find some horses."

"Morning'll be too late. Start looking around for loose boards in the walls . . . maybe a place where we could dig under . . . a tunnel. And while you're at it, keep your eyes peeled for something to use as weapons . . . wheel spokes, piece of a wagon, anything like that."

The men separated, began to prowl the dark interior of the barn. Adam, with Joe Denver at his side, went first to the rear where he made a careful but quiet examination of the door.

It was locked from the outside by a hasp and peg, he thought, but was not sure. Peering through a crack he saw that he was right; he also located the sentry, standing directly in front of the double panels.

He checked each of the windows. Both were small and high in the walls. They could forget them insofar as an escape route was concerned—and Griswold had wasted the men he stationed beneath them. The front entrance was similar to the back.

"We even rattle a board they're going to hear us," Denver said when they returned to the runway. "Don't hardly see how . . ."

"Wonder what's above?" Rait said, looking up.

"Loft, I reckon," the teamster said, and then brightened. "Sure. Ought to be doors at both ends so's they can throw in hay. Ought to be a ladder, too."

A dry squealing was issuing from one of the stalls. Adam crossed to investigate the sound. Two of the crew were working at a feed bin above the manger, tearing out the iron bars that controlled the quantity of hay fed into the box below. They paused as Rait halted behind them.

"Here's our weapons," Zeke Kelly said, tapping one of the rods. "Got 'em in every stall."

"Good . . . only go easy. We don't want that racket bringing in the soldiers."

There were three of the iron lengths to each

bin, and six stalls: eighteen half-inch bars about three feet long. Over half the teamsters would be armed, and with far better weapons than guns, under the circumstances. Whatever they did would have to be done silently, otherwise Cook's entire command would be down on them again.

"Ladder's here," Joe Denver called softly from across the runway.

Adam hurried to where the teamster waited. Unhesitating, he began to climb, placing his feet on the rungs close to the upright, not trusting the dry, splintered wood in the center. Reaching the loft, he pulled himself through the opening, stirring up a small cloud of choking dust. Denver, grunting and sweating, followed.

Streaks of light marked the location of the doors at both front and rear. Adam touched the teamster's arm. "Let's try the back."

They moved toward it slowly, taking each step with care, endeavoring to avoid loose boards that might squeak and alert the sentries outside the building. Reaching the door, little more than half full size, Adam halted, placed his hand against the cracked wood, and tested it gently. It moved an inch, hung. Exploring the right side of the panel, he found the trouble; a double length of baling wire had been passed through a hole in the door and secured to a staple in the facing; it would be simple to release.

The danger would lie in the screech of

undoubtedly rusty hinges when they were disturbed. The sentry was directly below, and to hope he would not hear was wishful thinking.

Adam gave it some thought, and then again touching Denver, retreated to the ladder. He started to descend, changed his mind, and made his way to the front of the loft. Ignoring the door, he crossed to a corner and placed his eye to a crack that afforded him a view of the street.

Jonesburg was going full swing; the saloons and the general store were open, and soldiers and civilians alike were milling about in the dusty haze that hung over the roadway.

Rait observed the activity in silence, wondering where Cook had quartered his men. The town itself was not large enough to accommodate them all, that was apparent; he and the teamsters had been placed in the only vacant building of sufficient size.

The flicker of several campfires drew his attention as his glance swept laterally across the town. He nodded in satisfaction. The soldiers were bivouacked along the eastern edge of the settlement, and the wagons were to the west. Once out of the barn they would not be compelled to pass near the camp. Turning, he moved back to the ladder and followed Denver to ground level.

He found the men waiting. They had removed the bars, and those who were not thus equipped had provided themselves with clubs salvaged from the destroyed feed bins.

"Reckon we're ready as we'll ever be," a man with a savagely scarred face said. "How we doing it?"

"Wait," Adam replied. "Street's full of soldiers. Let things quiet down."

"I thought you was in such an all-fired hurry?"

Adam could barely make out Bill Gannon's features in the dim light. "I am. We've got to be a long way from here by daylight if we expect to shake Cook . . . but we've got to get out of this barn first."

"How long before we can start?"

"The colonel strikes me as being one to go by the book. He'll have them all bugled in pretty quick, I'd guess. Then we make our move."

"How're we doing it?"

"Simple, but touchy," Rait said. "We need one man to go up into the loft, open the back door, and drop down on the sentry. It'll take somebody who can move quietly."

"That's me," Kiowa Jack Green said promptly. "I shed my boots, ain't no catamount living can walk softer."

"You're it, then. The moment you knock out the guard, open the runway doors . . . even if you hear the other guards coming. We can't help you if we're still locked in."

"They'll get opened," Kiowa Jack said. "You-all just be ready."

"What kind of weapon you got?"

The teamster held out a short length of wood shaved to roundness; it was a part of a broken singletree.

"Wouldn't want nothing better . . . 'cepting maybe my old knife."

The quavering notes of "Taps" floated sweetly through the night. Kiowa Jack bent and began to remove his boots.

"Thirty minutes yet," Adam said. "Give them time to settle down."

It was nearer an hour when Earl Handy, watching from the street-side door, passed word to Adam that all lights were out and there was no one to be seen.

Kiowa Jack moved to the ladder. Rait had briefed him on the bailing wire latch, and cautioned him also as to the probability of the hinges squeaking.

"Just you leave it to me," the old man said. "Little gob of tobacco spit'll work fine."

"Which way do we go when we get outside?" someone asked in a tense whisper.

"Wagons are west of us. That's straight ahead."

"Going to be open ground outside them doors. Is there any cover close?" someone else asked.

"Won't know the answer to that until Kiowa gets his job done."

"What about them guards standing watch at the wagons? Not forgetting them, are you?"

"No, but they shouldn't give us any trouble. Twice as many of us as there are guards. We'll cross that creek when we get to it. Everybody set?"

Metal squeaked faintly at the rear of the barn, Adam wheeled, alarm racing through him. Maybe Cook was back—making a final check. Rait watched the double doors swing back slowly to admit a flood of starlight. Outside he saw the sentry lying facedown, unmoving.

Chapter Seventeen

Stilling the murmur of surprise that ran through the men, Rait motioned for them to remain, and stepped to the doorway.

It could be some sort of trap. But that thought faded quickly when he saw the broad stain of blood covering the sentry's back. There could be only one answer—they had a friend in the settlement, or among the soldiers. It didn't make much sense, but the guard was there—and he was very dead.

Halting just within the door frame, Adam looked around carefully. There was no sign of the other sentries. The town lay, dark and silent, to his left. Without turning, he raised his arm, beckoned to the waiting teamsters. They came forward at once, pulled up around him.

"Leave one at a time," he said in a low voice. "Wait there," he added, pointing to a clump of trees on the far side of the cleared ground. "Joe . . . stick with me."

The crew began to leave the doorway, each man delaying until the one preceding him had gained the shelter of trees. One paused long enough to snatch up the dead soldier's rifle.

"When they're all across," Rait explained to

Joe Denver, "we'll close the doors and try to make it look like nothing's wrong."

"With him laying there?" the teamster said, pointing at the sentry.

Adam stopped one of the crew to relieve him of his iron bar. Stepping back into the barn, he entered the first stall, and, wedging the length of metal between two thick planks, bent it into a double hook.

Returning to Denver, he waited until the last man was across, then closing the doors quietly, he slipped the peg into the hasp.

"Help me hoist the guard."

Together they lifted the man, brought him to the doors. While Denver held the body upright, Adam placed the top hook in a convenient knothole, and then suspended the sentry from the lower.

The man's head sagged forward and his arms hung limply. Close examination would reveal quickly that he was dead, but from a distance—from the corners of the barn—he would appear to be slumped against the wall, sleeping.

"Let's go," Adam murmured urgently when the job was finished. "Pushed our luck pretty far as it is."

He waited until the stocky teamster had vanished into the shadows, and with a final glance at the quiet settlement followed hurriedly. Talk was running wild when he reached the men.

"Who do you reckon put that toad-stabber into the soldier?" was the first question to greet him.

Rait shook his head. "Anybody's guess. But he sure did us a favor. Move on. We've got no time to waste hashing it over."

He pushed through the men, taking his bearings from the scatter of houses, and struck off at a fast walk. Behind him the crew continued to speculate.

"Had to be somebody from town."

"Hell, that don't make no sense. Was the town that told that prissy colonel where we was."

"Could've been one of his soldiers, doing it for cussedness."

"That don't hold water, neither. As I recollect, they wasn't exactly friendly."

It was a matter of no concern to Adam Rait. They were free, and that's all that counted. Free for the time being anyway. If they were lucky and the escape wasn't discovered until morning, they'd have a chance. But only a chance, keeping fifteen wagons and a string of horses from the sharp eyes of fifty free-riding cavalrymen would be quite a chore.

They reached the camp and halted in a narrow ravine a few yards above the horses. Rait put his attention to locating the guards. The fire had been kept up and the area was well lit. He had no difficulty in pointing out the soldiers to the crew. Some were leaning against the wagons, dozing, but the majority were awake.

"Two men to each sentry," he murmured, drawing the teamsters around him. "Move in close so's you can jump your man fast. Use the iron bars . . . and don't let any of them pull a trigger. One gunshot will bring Cook down on us in a hurry."

"How'll we know when to move in?" Gannon asked.

"Watch the campfire. I'll circle around and walk in from the yonder side. When you see me stop, that'll be your signal."

Denver nodded his understanding. "You figure to keep the guards looking at you?"

"That's what I'm hoping for. Get at it. We're losing time."

Twenty men glided off into the shadows leaving Sancho, the boy Felipe, One-Eye Johnson, and Malachi Lee behind with Rait.

"You want us going with you?" the bearded Kentuckian asked.

"Best you sit tight here. Too many of us showing up at the fire would make them suspicious."

Adam waited out a full five minutes, allowing the men to get set, and then, ducking low, followed the ravine to its end, and cut right into the trees. Pausing there, he took a deep breath and walked boldly into the circle of firelight. Instantly a deep voice challenged him.

"Halt! Who's there?"

The nearest sentry peered at him from across

the flickering flames. Adam raised his arms high, continued to advance. He was taking swift count of the soldiers, wanting to be certain no change in number had been made and that he had drawn the attention of all.

"You hear? Halt, or I'll shoot!"

Ten men. All accounted for. Coming to a stop, he said: "Friend."

At that moment, all ten sentries went down, struck from behind by a teamster, while his partner leaped forward to catch the falling rifle preventing its accidental discharge. The scheme had gone off like clockwork.

Pleased, Rait hurried to the wagons. Sancho, and the others who had waited in the ravine, came up, and there was a burst of excited conversation.

"Get your weapons . . . over in the supply wagon," Adam said, cutting the talk short. "Soon as you do that, get hitched up."

Within three quarters of an hour the sentries had been securely trussed and gagged and the wagons made ready to roll. Rait, astride his bay, rode to where Denver and Ben Tipton waited in the lead wagon.

"The river's on ahead, about five miles. Keep them coming fast."

"We above or below a ford?"

"Don't know for sure," Adam replied. "I'll have a look. Just head out. I'll let you know in time."

They were above, and in a few minutes he returned and guided Denver and the others toward the shallow part of the stream, halting, however, a good hundred yards short of the water.

"What's the trouble?" Denver asked, standing up.

"I've got an idea how we might draw Cook off our trail when he comes rushing down here in the morning. Not much cover the way we'll be going, just low hills and brush. He'll spot us or our dust quick . . . unless we can turn him into the wrong direction."

The rest of the teamsters came trotting up, wondering at the halt. Rait turned to them. "Unload the last wagon. Scatter the cargo among the others, and be damned sure its lashed down tight."

The men stared. Darby Sims said: "What're you wanting to do?"

"Don't waste time asking questions!" Adam snapped. "Get at it!"

Denver dropped from his high perch. "I know you're in a powerful hurry, but I got to be told what you're figuring on."

"I want you to take the empty wagon and head south down the river. Felipe'll drive one of the supply wagons and follow close behind you. I'll take the train on across and keep going west."

"Meaning you're trying to make Cook think the whole works turned south, that it?"

Rait nodded. "We'll brush out the tracks leading down to the water, leave the ones you make when you turn. If Cook looks sharp, he'll see there's only the tracks of two wagons, but I'm guessing he's going to be in such a hurry he'll take the bait."

Joe Denver nodded. "I'll help that along a mite. I'll tie me some brush on the back of my rig, stir him up plenty of dust to see."

"Good. How long you think you can keep him busy?"

Denver looked off down the river. "Looks pretty flat and there's cover. We'll be traveling fast and empty. Ought to hold him for a day."

"If you can," Adam said slowly, "we'll be rid of him for good."

"Figure on it," Denver said. "Where you want me to meet you?"

"Once you've got him off your back . . . after you've taken him far as you can . . . cut due west. You'll hit the road to Tupelo. We'll be on it. Dust will show you where."

Denver glanced over his shoulder. "Boys've about got their moving done. Want me to take the train across?"

"Be obliged. Swing right, in behind that brush, once you're over. I'll get Felipe busy unloading his rig."

Denver climbed back onto his wagon as Rait whirled away. Raising his arm, he shouted the signal to move out. The heavily loaded vehicles rolled forward, dipped down into the shallow riverbed, crawled up the opposite sloping bank. As the last freighter came to a halt, Adam rode up.

"Every man down! Cut yourself some branches, start wiping out those tracks! Both sides of the river."

The teamsters hastened to comply. Only one, Red Lester, paused, looked up sullenly.

"You're sure in one hell of a danged rush."

"You'd better be, too," Rait snapped. "If we're not far enough away from here by daylight to keep Cook from spotting our dust, we're done for!"

Back on the opposite side of the river Joe Denver and Felipe were climbing into their wagons. The teamster gathered up his leathers, kicked off the brake, and shouted his team into motion. The boy swung in behind. Both vehicles rolled forward until they were within a dozen paces of the water, and then curved off to the south.

Denver lifted his hand in salute. "See you in church!" he shouted, and whipped his horses into a gallop.

Immediately Adam signaled Bill Gannon, now on the lead freighter. "Get 'em out of here, and don't slow down, come hell or salvation."

Chapter Eighteen

It was a hard day. Forsaking the marked roads and keeping to open country as he did, Rait found traveling slow. The ground was sandy and despite the unusually wide tread of the wagon wheels, the tires bit deep. Several times the drivers were forced to bring in the extra horses and double-team their rigs as they wormed their way through the low hills.

To make matters more disagreeable a hot wind off the Llano de los Cristanos, far to the south, sprang up around midafternoon and quickly built itself into a full-scale blast of sweeping clouds of stinging sand and choking dust in seemingly endless gusts.

But it was worth it, Adam thought, as he wiped grit from his lips and rubbed at his inflamed eyes. The efforts of Joe Denver and Felipe, combined with his own determination to keep the wagon train rolling at its best possible speed across the broken land despite the protests of some of the teamsters, had paid off. There was no sign of Zeb Cook and his renegade army.

He wished it were possible to keep the freighters moving on through the night and put more miles between them and the river. By that hour the Confederate leader and his cavalrymen would have realized their error, doubled back, and now be ranging wide in search. But it was out of the question. Both horses and men needed rest.

Accordingly, near sundown, Rait signaled for a halt in a deep swale. It wasn't a choice location, being overgrown with clumps of creosote bush and prickly pear cactus, but he could locate nothing better.

Mercifully the wind had died by the time camp was established and the tired horses cared for. They were deep in the short hills and likely far from Cook and his scouts, but Adam Rait still elected to play it safe; he ordered no campfire and permitted only a small blaze for the use of Sancho in preparing the meal.

Conversation during supper turned naturally to the escape from the barn and to the identity of their mysterious benefactor. A few were convinced that it was one of the townsmen, others still believed it to be a disgruntled soldier disliking the high-handed manner of Zebulon Cook and taking personal satisfaction.

"Well," Jeremy Haskins observed, drinking whiskey as a substitute for Sancho's acorn coffee in washing down his food, "I ain't for looking no mule in the mouth when he's give to me. We're here, and I'm plumb tickled about that."

Adam remained silent, listening to the various opinions expressed. He was too tired to think much about it, and, like Haskins, he was just thankful they had managed to escape. Someday, perhaps, they would learn who had done them the turn, and proper thanks could be made. At the moment he had more pressing matters to consider such as continuing to elude Cook. He hoped their luck would hold.

"Riders coming!"

The warning broke from one of the four posted sentries. Adam sprang to his feet, nerves tightening. Had he congratulated himself too soon?

"Spread out," he ordered in a hushed voice. "Hold your fire until I give the word. This time Cook's not taking us."

The teamsters melted into the brush shadows. Adam stepped back beyond the fire's glow. The odds would be more than two to one against them—almost three, in fact. He had a flashing recollection of his time of war, swore bitterly, helplessly. Things never changed.

And then Angela de Acera, accompanied by her brother, rode into view.

Hernando ducked his head politely. The light of the flames was red on his dark face. *"Buenas noches, señor."*

Frowning, Adam stepped forward, eyes on Angela. There was a change. She now wore more practical clothing, suitable for the trail, but it detracted none from her beauty. Abruptly he remembered the common courtesies.

"Step down. Sancho'll fix you a bite of supper."

"Muchas gracias," Hernando muttered, and came off his horse. The teamsters began to reappear.

Rait crossed to the girl. She swung down easily, her slender body lithe and graceful. One of the crew sighed audibly, admiringly. She faced Adam, smiling. "Our presence surprises you?" she asked in Spanish.

"Little surprises me any more. What of Fort Worth?"

Angela moved her shoulders. "It became necessary to abandon the journey."

Sancho stepped up, handed each a plate of food. He bowed, said apologetically: "I grieve that we have no chocolate, my lady."

"It is unnecessary. Is there water?"

"Yes, my lady," the old man replied, and scurried back to the chuck wagon.

Angela began to eat. The teamsters, puzzled also by the reappearance of the pair, lurked about in the shadows, listened. Bill Gannon broke the hush. He addressed Hernando.

"See anything of some soldiers . . . cavalry? Be about fifty in the bunch."

The Mexican nodded. "By the river. They look for you, no?"

"Just what they're doing. Had us cooped up in a barn, but we got loose."

Adam was studying the man closely. "You know about that?"

Hernando shrugged, made no answer. Gannon swept the teamsters with a knowing look. "Maybe I'm getting me an idea who that friend of ours was."

Rait considered. It was possible—except there was no logic behind it. Why would Hernando risk his neck to save theirs? But ahead of that one were other questions: What brought the de Aceras to them? Why hadn't they continued on to Fort Worth?

"Them soldiers," said Rufus Moore, "they heading this way?"

"They were near the river. They were not moving."

"When was that, *señor*?"

"Two, perhaps three hours before darkness."

Joe Denver had done a good job. Evidently Cook spent most of the day in a useless pursuit. Relief flowed through Adam. With so large a lead he should be able to keep the wagon train beyond the renegades' reach. And there would be no wheel tracks for them to follow, thanks to the wind from the Cristanos. He would like to think they had seen the last of Colonel Zebulon Cook, C.S.A., rejuvenated.

But none of this explained the presence of Angela and her brother. Rait waited while they continued to eat. The teamsters expected an emergency, and dead beat from the day's labor began to drift off to seek their blankets.

Adam, equally weary, had other matters on his mind. The de Aceras were there for a purpose, he was sure—just as there had been a reason for their joining the train in the beginning. A vague suspicion began to grow: if he knew for certain that it had been Hernando who struck down the sentry in Jonesburg, he would be close to the answer. Likely Hernando would deny it, if asked. Best to bide his time, let them make the first move.

"Where do you go?" he asked, still in Spanish when they returned their plates to Sancho. "You are far from well-traveled roads."

Angela was staring into the fire. Her face was a pale, soft oval, her eyes dark. "We have come to find you."

Adam leaned over, picked up a small branch, and tossed it into the flames. He had guessed right. He was certain of it now.

"You flatter me, my lady," he said with dry sarcasm, "but I see no purpose."

"There is important purpose," Hernando stated, pointing to the wagons. "We would buy the cargo you transport."

Rait's earlier conclusion left him bereft of surprise. He merely said: "Maximilian?"

"Maximilian, and a greater Mexico," Hernando said in a grand tone.

"That is questionable." Adam turned his eyes to Angela. "You are agents of the Royalists. Are you also brother and sister?"

"A matter of convenience only. A necessity."

"Your pardon, my lady," Hernando broke in. "Permit me to make the proper introductions." He bowed low to the girl. "The *Señorita* Angela de Acera . . . as you know. And I . . . I have the honor to be General Hernando Bernal, of His Majesty's loyal Mexican Brigades and Imperial Guard."

Angela displayed a frazzled annoyance at Bernal's grandiloquence. "It was arranged to meet with Kurt Hanover. Our intentions were to deal with him for the cargo. Unfortunately it was not accomplished."

"Unfortunately for him," Adam said coldly. "Was it necessary that he be murdered?"

She made a small motion with her hand. "Plans do not always go as expected. Had he lived it is possible an agreement could have been made."

"That's doubtful. He was a man of his word."

"Perhaps, but the ending of the North American war voided the promise."

"We speak of the dead," Hernando murmured. "Who is to say what a man would have done? It is better that we yet living conduct matters according to our own discretion."

Adam Rait felt the girl's eyes upon him, searching out his expression, endeavoring to penetrate his thoughts. *She's still beautiful in that get-up,* he told himself, and then realized she likely hoped he felt so; it was a part of her arsenal of persuasion.

"You are the inheritor of the cargo," Bernal said, coming to the point. "Are you of open mind?"

"It belongs to all of us . . . all of the teamsters. We share alike. I am owner of no greater portion than the others, although I serve as master of the train. As to the other, I have made my position clear to your associate."

He did not say Angela by name, but referred to her in the genderless term, as would two parties conferring on a business proposition.

Her head came up slightly and she said: "The general is aware of your feelings for Benito Juárez."

Bernal raised his hands, held them palms outward. "A matter of so vital importance should not be dismissed lightly."

"It has been dismissed. An agreement has been made with the Juárez government and a partial payment made. My word has been given."

The officer frowned. "To whom?"

"An agent of Juárez, Emiliano Escobar."

Bernal was visibly startled. "You have made such arrangements with this man . . . in person?"

"I have," Adam replied, wondering at Hernando's surprise. Understanding came to him. It had been one of Bernal's underlings who had attempted the ambush on the Juárista and Joe Denver.

He smiled. "Your man failed, General."

It was a shot in the dark, but Bernal was an old hand at deception. He only shrugged.

149

"Your meaning is not clear. Regardless, it is difficult to understand how you consider it necessary to observe honor when dealing with revolutionists . . . outlaws who defy lawful authority."

"A matter of opinion. Nevertheless, it would have been Hanover's decision also to sell to the Juáristas."

Bernal sighed. "Again we speak in supposition."

"No. I was with him when he made such a statement. He had no liking for the Maximilian government and thought well of Benito Juárez."

Hernando Bernal stirred impatiently. "Of what concern is Mexico to you? What matters who governs? Is gold not of the greatest importance? It is my intention to pay an even higher price for the cargo. Does that not interest you?"

Adam Rait shook his head.

The general's face darkened. "You are most unwise. . . ."

Rait laughed. "A threat, my friend? Perhaps you will eliminate me as you did Kurt Hanover. I think not. It is said in your country that when a man knows where the scorpion crawls, he is never bitten. Thus I shall be wary."

"Your decision, then, is final?"

"It is. I have made an agreement with the Juárez government. I will fulfill it."

Chapter Nineteen

Hernando Bernal cast a sideward glance at Angela, allowed his shoulders to slump.

"So be it . . . it is useless for me to say more. With your kind permission, however, we shall remain with you until the border of my country is reached. A matter of protection for the lady, Angela."

"Is there not a different reason, General?"

The officer frowned. "I do not understand."

So your lady Angela can try her tricks on me, Adam was about to reply, but let it go. Instead he said: "It is nothing. Merely a passing thought. You are welcome to ride with us, but I assure you now, further conversation on the matter of the cargo is useless."

"As you will, but perhaps . . ."

"It is finished," Rait said flatly, and turned to Angela. "A bed will be made for you in the supply wagon."

"Do not trouble yourself," she said coolly. "I shall find a place under the trees."

"Not while I've got twenty or so teamsters scattered about in the brush," he snapped, forgetting his Spanish. "Or maybe you'd like that?"

She gave him a quiet, infuriating smile, and he wheeled suddenly away and strode to the wagon.

It was almost empty, and Adam pushed what remained aside and, unrolling a fold of blankets, whipped them into a pallet. Still angry, he stepped back, turned. That would take care of her, and if he slept somewhere nearby, she should be both comfortable and safe. Bernal could do what he damned well pleased. He looked up and found Angela standing before him.

"It's ready," he said.

Her reply was a quiet—"Thank you."—as she climbed, unaided, into the vehicle.

He remained motionless, surprised at the gentleness of her manner, and then recalling his previous assumption that this was all a part of her inventory of cunning, he whirled, stalked to the dwindling fire.

Rigid, he paused there, suddenly far from sleep. His mind was turbulent, skipping from thoughts of the luckless Hanover to Zeb Cook and his misguided followers; to Joe Denver and Felipe—and the hope that they had not fallen victim to the officer's ungovernable anger; to Escobar and the Juárista escort that could not arrive too soon; to Hernando Bernal, and to Angela. . . .

He lit a cigar, took a few puffs, and finding the weed tasteless, dropped it into the dull embers. Angela—damn her—why did she have to be what she was? Why did she have to come back? Why? He thrashed it about for some time and then, giving it up, sought his blankets.

• • •

The train was under way at sunrise. Adam, making his customary rounds, saw little of Angela and Bernal and left it up to them to seek out their breakfasts and prepare for the day's journey. They took positions to the left, he noted, thus avoiding dust. It was a good place, well removed from where he rode at the head of the column. In the mood that gripped him he did not want them near.

His warning to Bernal that henceforth he would be on guard against the fate that had tripped up Kurt Hanover had not been idle talk. That the Mexican officer was a ruthless, determined man was evident. He had killed Hanover; Adam was convinced of it now. That he had also engineered the attempt on Emiliano Escobar's life was likewise apparent.

And the death of the Jonesburg sentry? Bernal would have realized all hope for obtaining the shipment of rifles and ammunition would be lost once Zeb Cook took possession. Accordingly he had felt compelled to make escape possible for the teamsters. Once free with the cargo in their hands, there was a chance to negotiate.

He considered Angela. It was hard to believe she was involved in it all—a partner in the killings that had been committed. She was—by association—yet there was to her an indefinable quality that bespoke a resoluteness of purpose, a strange sort of courage that nullified the

153

ruthlessness of Hernando Bernal and prevented its rubbing off on her. He wished to hell he could understand her—or his own private thoughts of her, for that matter.

The knowledge that Bernal had been responsible for the attack on Escobar disturbed him. Martinez, or whoever had been assigned to do the job, could have made a second attempt and succeeded. One thing he must do, he decided. When Joe Denver returned, he would send him on to Tupelo, have him contact the Juáristas, make certain an escort would be on its way. It might prove a useless ride for the teamster as Escobar could have gotten through—but it was best to be certain.

Late in the morning he called a halt in a thin stand of trees scattered about a spring. The day was hot and he had pushed the teams hard, so he deemed it prudent to pause for an hour in the cooling shade and rest. They were also drawing near Comanche country and he wanted the men to be aware of the danger.

The word passed. He took advantage of the break to shift his gear from the bay to Hanover's black, which had been having an easy time of running with the remuda. The bay had been in almost constant use since the beginning.

When the break was over, he again took his place ahead of the lead wagon. Shortly Angela rode up beside him.

Oddly he felt no resentment when he looked at her; he actually became aware of a pleasure at having her company.

He grinned, said: "Does all go well with the Steel Angel?"

Annoyance crossed her features. "Please continue to speak in English. I'm tired of being Spanish."

He brushed his hat to the back of his head, again, smiled. "That's progress. Maybe you're getting fed up with the whole Mexican problem."

She stirred, looked off through the trees to where the land rose and fell in an endless carpet of shimmering sand. "It's hard to give up a way of life."

"Hard to give up anything that's part of you."

She turned her head, studied him soberly. "It sounds as though you had once lost something important . . . perhaps very dear to you."

"Who hasn't? Everybody gives up something. Living is a give and take proposition, and no bed of feathers for any man . . . or woman. There are the things you want, that you'd like to be . . . and there's that which you finally settle for."

"I never realized you were so bitter."

He shook his head impatiently. "Not bitter, just everyday practical. Best you learn to face reality early."

"Reality," she echoed forlornly. "A poor word.

What does it mean? How can you tell when you face it?"

"You are . . . right now. You just haven't the guts to admit it."

"Me? How?" There was genuine surprise in her tone. "In what way?"

"Betting your money . . . actually your life . . . on Maximilian. He can't win. People of Mexico will never hold still for an outsider running their country. They'll turn the place inside out until they're rid of him, along with all those backing him."

"Why? What does it matter who sits on the throne of any country? It's the men who actually run the government that make the decisions."

"No doubt, but they reflect the thinking of the man, or woman, at the head. And the Mexicans have had all the kings they can swallow. They've had a taste of what's called representative government and they'll fight until they get it back. Admitting to yourself that's true when you don't want to accept it is reality."

He glanced at her. She was watching him closely, with an odd, soft light in her eyes, as if she were smiling, but not with her lips.

"You think a lot of the Mexican people, don't you?"

"Always have. Learned to know and understand them years ago. Someday, when things settle down, I'd like to move to Mexico, build myself a ranch over Chihuahua way . . . good cattle country in some parts."

Adam twisted, braced himself with one hand on the cantle, and looked back over the train. It was strung out in an almost perfectly straight line, with the wagons closely bunched under their canopy of thin dust. Bernal, he noticed, was on the seat beside Bill Gannon, evidently taking some relief from the saddle.

"I see why you're so determined to get your cargo to Juárez," Angela said. "You might say you have a reason for seeing him regain power."

"I only said I'd like to have a ranch there," Adam replied, resuming his position. "Not much prospect of it ever happening. What about you? If Maximilian loses out, what will you do?"

"I've not thought that far ahead. We'll lose our land . . . our home, of course. The new government will confiscate everything owned by those who support Maximilian."

"That's not all they'll do," Rait said quietly, "if I'm any judge of how the Mexican people feel."

"I realize that. Perhaps that's why I haven't thought about it . . . but everything's a risk. Either you win or you lose . . . and if you lose your way of life, what's left?"

"People of the South . . . the Confederacy . . . are facing that right now. They'll go on living, try to make a new way of life. What else is there to do?"

"At least they won't be stood before a wall and shot."

He grinned at her. "Best way to avoid that is change horses while there's still time."

"Like the old saying about rats deserting a sinking ship. Only how can you be sure the ship's sinking?"

"So we're back to facing reality. You should be convinced. Juárez gets stronger every day, and when your friend Napoleon pulls out his army, Maximilian's government will blow sky high."

She nodded. "It is known that your President Lincoln and Benito Juárez are *sympatico*. Will he help the Juáristas now that your war is over?"

"I expect he'd like to."

"I've heard it said that Juárez copies everything he does from Lincoln . . . even to wearing a silk hat."

"Could be. But I'm afraid Juárez won't get much help from him. He's got problems of his own."

A shout of laughter erupted from the train. Adam looked over his shoulder. Bernal was now riding on the second wagon, sitting atop the cargo. Several teamsters, taking their break from driving, were gathered around him. Gannon's relief driver, Ben Tipton, had assumed the leathers of the lead team. Where Bill was Rait could not tell.

"Your general seems to be quite a yarn spinner," Adam said, turning back.

"As are most soldiers."

Rait cast an eye at the sun. "Known him long?"

"Oh, I've seen him around the palace, off and on, for three or four years. He's a pure-blood Spaniard, from the San Luis Potosi country."

"Got connections with the high-ups, I take it."

"Not really. He's a professional soldier . . . and not very happy, I'm afraid, with this particular assignment."

"It hasn't prevented his carrying it out," Adam said dryly. He was thinking of Hanover, and Escobar, and the sentry at Jonesburg.

Angela brushed at her face. "I don't condone what he did . . . or didn't do . . . and I'm not always aware of his actions. But, as I've said, he's a professional and he does what he must."

"If I get the chance, I'll turn him over to the law for murder," Rait said, again glancing at the sun. Abruptly he turned, cupped his hands to his lips. "Whip up! Getting late!"

"What about me?" Angela asked. "Will you hand me over to your law, too?"

"Why not? You're a part of it, aren't you?"

"I guess so. But murder was no part of the bargain. I thought . . ."

She was far from a woman of steel in that moment, Adam thought, looking at her. The remoteness had vanished and there was a loneliness about her. But for him it changed nothing.

"Everybody makes mistakes," he said, "and pays for them. It's a rule nobody ever gets around. The worst of it is that the mistakes we make never stop haunting us . . . until something happens to wipe them out."

"Like being stood up before a firing squad?"

"That's what I mean. You got into this thing because it all sounded exciting, maybe romantic. It was your big chance to become a hero . . . heroine . . . your name on everybody's lips. A new Joan of Arc and all that."

As his tone became progressively harsh, she turned to him, frowning. Her lips pulled into a firm line.

"It was all to be a great adventure . . . only you overlooked the dirty side of it . . . and you forgot to ask yourself who was right and who was wrong. Now you're having second thoughts and wishing you were out of it, that you'd never started. . . ."

"No!" she cried, pulling up abruptly, stiff and outraged. "You're . . . you're . . ."

Whatever she intended to say was left unfinished, for just as suddenly, she whirled and spurred away.

Adam watched her cut back toward the rear of the train. Her unexpected flight had startled him, taken him unawares, and then he guessed he had it coming; he had been rough with her—but then, she deserved it.

Once more he glanced to the sky; the sun would be down within the hour. He was still prodded by a need to keep rolling, put as much land between the train and Zeb Cook as possible, but horseflesh had its limit, and there was harness that needed repairing. He began to look for a suitable camp-site, decided on a broad plain a quarter mile to the south.

He rode on ahead, reached the flat, and gave the signal to circle in for the night. Bernal, now riding on the last wagon, dropped to the ground and mounted his trailing horse. Sancho swung the chuck wagon off to one side, climbed down with an old man's stiffness, shouted something to the driver handling the supply rig.

Adam Rait waited until all had come to a halt, then rode the black to where the wrangler was stringing his rope corral and turned the horse over to him. Moving into the center of the circle formed by the freighters, he stood for a moment enjoying the rank, blending odors of rabbit-brush, dust, and trampled creosote bush, and then called off the names of the four men who were to take the first turn as sentries. He started to move on, paused.

The sentries showed no intention of assuming their positions. Angry, he swung his attention to where the teamsters had gathered around Bill Gannon.

"Cushman . . . Sims . . . Fouche . . . Lester!" he repeated the names. "Get out where you belong!"

Gannon advanced a few paces into the clearing. The crew followed slowly. Sancho hesitated, turned to watch. Farther over Angela and Hernando Bernal, still in their saddles, looked on in silence.

"Simmer down, Rait," Gannon said. "We're aiming to talk a bit."

Rigid, nerves taut as piano wire, Adam waited. He had no idea what the trouble might be, but far back in his mind something told him that Bernal was at the bottom of it.

Bill Gannon came to a stop a wagon length away. "Me and the boys," he said, his broad face flushed and belligerent, "have been doing some thinking . . ."

The teamster hesitated. Adam remained silent. Malachi Lee cleared his throat noisily. "Hell's afire, Bill. Get on with it," he said in a dry, dissatisfied way.

Gannon nodded. He hitched at his gun belt. "Like I told you, we been doing some thinking. We've decided to sell out to the general."

Chapter Twenty

Temper flared through Rait. Now he knew what Hernando Bernal had been up to—riding the wagons, talking to the crew, laughing, persuading them to his way of thinking . . . and Angela. He flung an angry glance to her. She had been a part of it, keeping him occupied while the Mexican general got himself in solid with the men. Adam saw her turn, say something to the officer, and then lower her head. He cut back to Gannon and the teamsters.

"You've decided?" he repeated softly.

"That we have. Took us a count. About every man was for it first time around. Them that wasn't come over when we done it again."

Adam restrained himself with difficulty as the urge to rush forward, smash his fists into Gannon's smirking face surged through him. He stood silent, allowed the anger to pass, his hard gaze raking the men slowly.

"What the hell's this all about?" he asked finally.

Ed Vernon stepped up beside Gannon. "Maybe Bill here didn't handle this thing just right, Cap'n. What he was meaning to tell you is that we been listening to General Bernal, and he's offering us a better deal. We figured it'd be smart to take it."

Rait's laugh was a harsh sound. "Better deal! Anything he'd offer you'd come up short."

"He's willing to pay fifty thousand for the cargo. Ten thousand more'n we're getting."

"And we won't be freighting it clear to Juárez City," Gannon added. "All we've got to do is head straight for the border. He's got drivers who'll take over when we get there."

Adam stared at the men incredulously. "What kind of damned fools are you?"

"For ten thousand more gold . . . ," Gannon began.

"You'll never see it . . . or any part of the rest you've been promised."

"How do you know?" Bill Gannon demanded. "You got some proof Bernal ain't on the square . . . and that the Juárez bunch is?"

"I know you can't trust Bernal. He was sent up here to get our cargo, one way or another. He killed Hanover, or had it done, when he got nowhere with him. Figured it would be easier to deal with me."

"He told us he never got no chance to talk to you. Said you cooked up a sale with Escobar before he could make an offer. That right?"

"You were there," Adam said. "But it wouldn't have mattered. I'd never have sold to him anyway . . . and neither would Kurt Hanover if he'd been alive."

"Why wouldn't you? Got some big reason?"

"The people Bernal represents have no right to be in Mexico. I'll have nothing to do with keeping them there."

Bill Gannon laughed. "Hear that, boys? He don't like the general's friends . . . so it costs us ten thousand dollars in gold. And a couple extra weeks on them hard tails."

"Hell with that!" Red Lester shouted. "I don't give a hoot who's running Mexico. I'm just looking to get paid."

He'd made a mistake taking the men in as partners at the beginning, Adam realized. It would have been better to wait until delivery was made and then divide the payment into equal shares. But at the time it seemed the best thing to do.

"Did you stop to figure what your cut of ten thousand will be . . . if you get it?" he said, trying to reason. "Less than five hundred apiece."

"Looks plenty big to me," Eli Jones said, biting a corner off his tobacco plug. "Man can do a lot with that much cash."

"And what about the deal we made with Escobar . . . the Juáristas? We took their money . . . and we gave Escobar our word . . . a promise . . . one they'll be relying on. You going back on that?"

"You fretting over a piddling two thousand? Hell, we'll give it back," Gannon said. "You got most of it left, anyway. Reckon we can afford to make up what's been spent."

"What about your word?"

"Ain't worrying none about that. Nobody's going to expect us to keep it when we give it to an outlaw . . . a greaser at that."

"But you'll take the word of Bernal. You don't make sense, Bill. None of you do," Rait added, looking at the men.

"We was hoping you'd see it our way," Darby Sims said, shaking his head. "Money means a lot. Most of us ain't never had much more'n the price of a drink in our pockets . . . and plenty of times we ain't had that."

"Then you'd better listen to me," Adam broke in. "With Bernal you'll lose it all. You'll never get paid a cent! Juárez will pay off. I'll stake my life on it. And you're forgetting something else . . . Zeb Cook."

Gannon spat, cocked his head to one side. "What about him?"

"Long as we keep going the direction we are, we're putting distance between us and his outfit. You swing due south and you'll make it easy for him to catch up."

Gannon snorted. "What makes you think he's still trailing us?"

"What makes you think he's not?"

A long minute of silence followed. Gannon shrugged. "Ain't a-feared of that. We keep rolling we'll make the border before that can happen."

"Another fool statement," Rait snapped. "You

think you can outrun a troop of cavalry? Use your head!"

"The big reason we was hoping you'd see things our way," Rufus Moore said, taking up where Sims had left off, "we need you to keep bossing things."

"Why should I?"

" 'Cause you got a right to be in on it," Rufus said, "maybe more'n the rest of us."

"Why didn't you think of that earlier and give me a chance to talk with Bernal?"

"Well, you said we was all pardners, sharing equal and all that. And there wasn't time to do nothing . . . not with you pushing us hard and the general saying we ought to be turning south if we aimed to take him up. So we voted and agreed. If you want, we'll do our voting again."

Adam shook his head wearily. "The way you've made up your minds, I don't figure it would change anything . . . and I can't make you see that it's a mistake."

"Ain't nothing changing our minds," Bill Gannon said. "Now, you aiming to stay with us? We're willing to let you run things, long as you do what we want."

"Turn south for the border?"

"That's it. You'll get your share when we're paid off. And we'll make up the difference so's you can trot that two thousand back to your friend in Juárez City, when it's all done. Take it or leave it."

Adam knew it was hopeless to argue. Teamsters were a hard-headed lot and all they could see was the extra $10,000 in gold, promised them by Hernando Bernal. They'd never see it . . . or any of the rest, he was certain.

But it was a long way to the border, and perhaps he had an ace in the hole. Gannon and the others seemed to have forgotten Joe Denver and Felipe. And chances were Bernal was totally unaware of their absence. If he could get in touch with Denver—assuming he still lived—before he returned to the train, he could detour him on to Tupelo for help. With luck they might rescue the wagons and their cargo before Hernando Bernal's men took over.

"Seems I don't have much choice," he said. "It's a mistake, but I'll string along."

Several of the teamsters yelled their approval. Bill Gannon, victorious, smiled broadly, extended his hand. "No hard feelings?"

Adam turned away, faced the teamsters. "All right, we're doing it your way. It still means the horses need tending and chores done. I want all the wheel hubs checked for grease. We'll have to roll fast if we aim to keep Cook off our backs."

The crowd broke up as the men started for their wagons. Rait came about, found Hernando Bernal, still mounted, standing behind him. The officer nodded.

"I am sorry, my friend. The fortunes of war, eh?"

Rait pinned the man with a cold stare. "Like the rattlesnake, you move quickly when my face is turned from you. A pity God did not give you rattles also that others might be warned."

The officer's smile remained fixed. He stirred slightly. "I am a soldier doing his duty."

"No . . . a murderer and a liar leading men to their deaths," Adam countered, and then in English said: "Now get the hell away from me . . . and stay away! The same goes for your doxie," he finished, pointing at Angela.

She sat in the warm darkness of the supply wagon and studied Adam Rait. He stood near the fire, down now to embers, staring off into the night. Except for the sentries stationed a distance from the camp, all of the other men were asleep.

She moved restlessly. Earlier she had been furious with him, at the harsh manner in which he had spoken to her, and at herself for her own failure to make him understand her position, her problems. But to Adam Rait everything was either black or white, and subtleties were as foreign to him as was Maximilian to Mexico.

She recalled how he had faced Gannon and the teamsters, standing there before them defiantly, while he fought with his will as he attempted to persuade them they were wrong, that they should not trust Bernal but stand by their promise to the Juáristas.

He was what the Mexican people called *macho*—a real man. Subconsciously she endeavored to compare him with the elegant dandies that hung around Maximilian's court: Rait stood tall, without actually being so, high above them, and the hard, clean lines of his features made the foppish gentlemen she once had thought gallant appear effeminate.

The way he carried himself, that limp that gave him a dashing, reckless air. How had he sustained it? Could it have been a duel over a woman? Angela smiled in the darkness. She was thinking like a schoolgirl, visualizing her idol, but there was a rough masculinity to him, a strength that differed from that associated with the strong. It set him apart and she was finding it impossible to dismiss him from her mind.

She wondered if he had ever married. He had not spoken of a wife—even of women as a passing fancy. That could mean nothing. She would like being his wife, or just his woman, she told herself, shamelessly frank in the safety of her own private thoughts.

But that was a hope she might as well forget. The way Adam Rait felt about her—still, there were some things he should know. That she had been an ignorant accomplice of Hernando Bernal's scheme that day, for one, and she should apologize for getting angry when he thought he was making her see the truth about herself.

170

Marshaling her courage, she climbed from the wagon, crossed to where he stood. He heard her coming, looked around, his face inscrutable.

"About today," she began hesitantly, "I . . . I know what you must think . . . about what Bernal did . . . but you're wrong. I had no part in it. I was with you because, well . . . because I wanted to be."

He turned his head again to stare off into the night. "Makes no difference. You're still in it."

Penetrating the defense he had thrown around himself was to Angela like hammering on a wall of stone. "Earlier, when you were giving me a look at myself . . . I was trying to make you understand something . . . things aren't always exactly the way they seem."

He did not move. Far back in the direction of the river a coyote yapped a shrill challenge.

"All the things you said were true," she continued almost desperately. "Or partly so. And a lot of it doesn't have much meaning to me . . . any more."

"It's a little hard to believe that."

"You don't think it's possible I could change?"

"I'd as soon expect hell to freeze," he said bluntly. "You trying to tell me you're no longer interested in preserving the great Maximilian and the gay life of Mexico City?"

She shrugged off the heavy sarcasm, remained silent.

"Figured that," he said. "And it's gone your way. Bernal worked a slicker on me and on the men. He got what you both wanted and there's damned little I can do to stop you now . . . but there is one thing I'm curious about."

Angela's head came up, hopefully. "Yes?"

"If he'd failed to swing the teamsters to his proposition, what would've happened next? Would you have come crawling into my blankets tonight ready to try your hand at persuading me?"

Angela recoiled. The urge to slap him raced through her, and then she realized he had every reason to voice the question. Anger rushed to her defense, tipped her tongue with venom.

"Possibly. . . . Had I . . . would you have agreed?"

Adam Rait stiffened perceptibly. It was as though he had expected that very answer, yet did not want to hear it.

"No," he said finally—and flatly.

"Are you sure? Would I be so hard to take?"

"Not that . . . far from it. But when and if you come into my arms, it has to be because you want to be there, not as a part of some god-damned business deal."

Rigidly he wheeled and strode off into the starlit night.

Words rushed to Angela's lips. She wanted to cry out, stop him, try to make him understand.

But it was too late—everything was too late.
Forget it. Forget him.

Turning slowly, she walked to the wagon and climbed into her bed.

Chapter Twenty-One

The days following moved by in routine fashion. Sunrise—the intervening hours of sweat, rolling hills, sandy flats, rumbling wagons and clanking chains, shouting teamsters, dust, inescapable heat—then sunset. And riding above it all like a gray cloud were the intangible threats: Zebulon Cook, savage Comanches, and, for Adam, the growing proximity of Hernando Bernal's Mexican brigades.

Throughout the devastating monotony Rait maintained his lonely isolation at the head of the column, faithful to his duties, and while civil in his relations with the teamsters, his mingling was limited, his manner definitely remote. As to Angela de Acera and Bernal, he was stonily indifferent, treating them as though they were nonexistent.

Eventually the plains country through which they were passing began to play out, and they entered a hilly land carved in haphazard abandon by frowning red bluffs and wide, sand-bottom washes. The wheels of the wagons bit deep into the loose surface, and progress slowed considerably. Adam counted it fortunate when they could cover fifteen miles in a twelve-hour day.

He began now to watch the southeast. Joe

Denver and Felipe should be putting in an appearance, such depending of course on how far off the trail they had led Zebulon Cook and his men—and if they were still alive.

That possibility had continually disturbed Rait despite his confidence in the husky teamster's ability to take care of himself, and he tried to keep it from his mind by assuring himself that Denver would return. Several times that particular day he rode to the crest of some convenient hill and spent minutes probing the horizon. On each occasion he saw nothing but empty, sprawling reaches of broken country.

Such activity eventually drew the narrow-eyed attention of Hernando Bernal, and late that afternoon he saw the officer pull off a short distance and stare into the same direction as though he, too, were expecting someone; Adam put it down to curiosity and suspicion on the part of the Mexican.

He had only a tentative plan for when Joe Denver returned. It would be necessary to spot him far in advance, and then ride out unnoticed to meet him before he could reach the wagons.

He would exchange the horse he rode for the wagon Denver would be driving, thus affording the teamster faster transportation. Speed in summoning the Juáristas would be all important by that time. Seeing him return with Denver's wagon would arouse immediate doubts on the part of Bill Gannon and the other teamsters, but by then it would be too late to do anything about it.

Hernando Bernal was something else. If he attempted to follow Joe, Adam was determined to stop him, with a gun, if necessary. But that was a side issue; the important thing was to catch Denver well before the crew knew of his coming—and that would require constant vigilance.

Around 4:00 p.m. of the next day he saw a faded, yellow ball take shape in the distant sky. It was no more than a discoloration but he knew it was dust, and it lay in the right direction. Once noted, Adam took pains to ignore it, fearful of drawing anyone's attention, but he began to look ahead to when he could slip away and determine if it was Joe Denver.

The bluffs and broad washes, interlaced with long weedy slopes, had become more prevalent. They were crossing country that could almost be termed brakes, and he realized, also, that they were not too distant from the border.

It was fortunate Denver was finally arriving—if Denver it were. Once the train fell into custody of Bernal's cavalrymen, the chances of wresting it back and conveying the cargo on to Juárez City would be very slim.

An hour later on the firm surface of a long slope he halted, raised his arm. "Pull in! Pull in!" he shouted. "Night camp!"

Immediately Bill Gannon, handing the reins to his relief driver, leaped from his seat and came running forward.

"What the hell's the matter?" the teamster yelled. "We got a couple hours left yet."

"We camp here," Adam answered firmly, and then added: "Maybe you'd like to take a vote?"

Gannon swore as the barb dug in, wagged his head. "Ought to make as far as we can."

"Not sure what's ahead," Rait said.

"Won't hurt none to keep going."

"Maybe not . . . but we're stopping here. Now, either get back and bring up that wagon, or I'll do it for you."

Gannon hung motionlessly for several moments of indecision, and then whirled, retraced his steps. Pulling himself up and onto the seat, he snatched the leathers from his partner, popped his long whip, and sent the freighter rumbling forward.

Adam stayed in the saddle, watched the wagons shape up, halt, and the teamsters turn to their chores. Sancho, finding a nearly level spot, brought his rig to a standstill, chocked the wheels with small rocks, and began to break out his equipment.

Only then did Adam Rait come about and drift slowly for the lower end of the slope. Ostensibly he was following his usual custom of having a last look at the country ahead over which the train would be crossing that next day. It was not uncommon and no one paid any attention to him—no one except Hernando Bernal.

He glanced at the officer and the girl when he passed the supply wagon that she still used as her personal quarters. He saw her standing there, one hand resting on the tailgate, regarding him in that cool way that always stirred him. He made no effort to speak, simply continued on. Bernal immediately stepped away from the vehicle, following him with his small sharp eyes.

Moments later Rait entered a steep-walled arroyo and, shielded from view of the camp, he cut left and began to move toward the now definite dust roll floating above the low hills. Keeping to the bed of the wash, winding in and out of clumps of feathery flowered Apache plume, scarlet-tipped ocotillo, and other wild growth, he broke finally onto a long slide that terminated a quarter mile away in a second, larger arroyo.

He could not see the exact source of the dust. Its origination seemed beyond a fairly high rise some distance on ahead. He began to wonder—the cloud appeared far too large for one stirred up by two wagons. But the country was powder dry, and four horses drawing two vehicles at considerable speed could conceivably churn up a substantial haze.

Rait heard the soft thud of an approaching rider at that moment, realized he had been trailed. He pulled off immediately, drew the bay in behind a clump of head-high doveweed. Hernando Bernal appeared. The officer was frowning, his gaze on the loose sand as he searched for prints left by Adam's mount.

"Looking for me, General?"

At Rait's question the officer jerked to a halt. His head came up and he stared at Adam. "I look for you," he said quietly in English.

"You found me. Now what?"

Bernal leaned forward. "Your heart is not with your words, *gringo*. You still oppose me and have plans of a personal nature."

"Reckon you're sort of a mind-reader," Adam drawled. "What about it?"

Hernando shrugged, lazily deceptive. "A solution is simple. You will die . . . here."

Suddenly, with the final word, he drove roweled spurs into his horse, sent the animal plunging ahead. A knife glittered in his hand.

Adam hauled back on the bay, bringing him to his hind legs. Bernal thundered by at close quarters. Rait struck out, using his balled fist as a club. The blow was only a glancing one but it caught the officer on the neck and rocked him off balance. His horse veered sharply to avoid the brush, and Hernando went sideways out of the saddle.

Rait, boiling with suppressed anger finally unleashed, was off the bay and on Bernal before

179

the man could recover. Wrenching the knife free, he hurled it into the brush, dragged the officer to his feet. Swinging hard, he drove a right to Bernal's jaw.

Hernando groaned, sank back. Heaving for breath, Adam towered over him. "Get up . . . god damn you! I'm not through yet!"

Bernal lunged, caught Rait around the ankles, pulled him down. Locked together, they thrashed about, half in, half out of the brush. Adam kicked free, sprang to his feet. Bernal came up with him.

He closed fast, throwing himself at Rait. Adam jumped aside, tripped, and again both were on the ground, hammering at one another's body. This was far different from the fight he had engaged in with Gannon. Bill, all muscle and strength, could take no shock to the jaw; however Hernando was somehow weathering everything Rait could throw.

Adam managed to get to his knees. Bernal's dark, sweaty face was rising up to him. Locking his hands together, Rait clubbed the man on the nose, heard bone crack, saw the officer fall away.

Rising, sucking deep for wind, Adam seized the officer's arm, hauled him half upright. Throwing his weight into a spin, he swung Bernal around, crashed him into the brush. The officer groaned and tried to recover his balance. Adam stepped in close, smashed a hard blow to the belly, another to the head. Drawing back, he allowed Bernal to fall, instantly dropped onto him and encircled the man's throat with his fingers.

"Anybody dies," he gasped, "it won't be me."

Motion far out on a plain beyond the hills caught his attention in that same moment; it was to the east. He frowned, glanced to the dust in the south. It looked like another party—Zeb Cook!

He recognized the body of men on second glance. There were fifty or more horsemen, strung out in a wide skirmish line. Cook was in the advance. Behind him rode two officers, likely Griswold and perhaps Slade, the sergeant.

A pace behind them came the flag bearer, supporting the banner of the Confederacy. Cook was moving up on the camp. Whether by accident or design, it was not possible to know. In either event, he would see the wagons in a short time.

Rait leaped to his feet, whirled to the bay, and vaulted onto the saddle. Ignoring Bernal, now sitting up, rubbing his throat, he spun and cut back up the arroyo at full gallop, recklessly swerving through the brush and shoulders of rock.

He came into camp at a rush. The sound of his approach had brought the teamsters to an alert and they stood grouped near the wagons, weapons drawn.

"Hitch up!" Adam shouted, bringing the bay to a sliding halt. "Cook and his bunch are closing in. Move, god dammit! Don't stand there gawking!"

Immediately the crew broke and ran to where the horses were picketed. Sancho began to throw his gear into the chuck wagon, yelling for someone to bring up his team. Rait, leaving the saddle, rushed to help.

From the corner of his eye Adam saw Angela hurriedly throwing gear onto her mount. They would have to forget the supply wagon; there was no time to waste on it.

"Where the hell we going?" Gannon shouted from across the clearing.

"High bluff . . . about two miles from here. Can't outrun Cook, so we'd best make a stand."

Gannon nodded, continued to work with his relief man at getting the team in harness. Shortly several of the freighters were ready to move.

Adam motioned to them. "Pull out! Don't waste time lining up!"

He jerked the last buckle tight, yelled at Sancho to whip up, and swung to the bay. The wagons were rolling by, wheels making sharp cutting sounds on the gravelly surface. Over to the left the wrangler was hazing the extra horses into a trot.

Rait went up into the saddle, glanced to where he had last seen Angela; surprise touched him. Bernal, looking dusty and rumpled, had returned. He was in earnest conversation with the girl.

Jamming spurs to his horse, Adam raced to get ahead of the freighters. Angela and Hernando Bernal would have to take care of themselves.

Chapter Twenty-Two

The wagons were strung out in a broken line up the slope leading to the bluff. The ground was firm, if rough, and the heavily loaded vehicles bounced and lurched from side to side as the teamsters, upright, legs braced, cracked their long whips and shouted at the straining horses.

Adam forged ahead of the lead freighter. It was driven by Rube Waterhouse. The man had lost his hat and his uncut hair was streaming in the breeze; his wagon was open, and Rait could hear a steady flow of affectionate cursing above the grumbling of his wagon.

Adam looked to the ridge where Zeb Cook would make his initial appearance. Two riders were silhouetted against the pearl-like sky—advance scouts. If the commander of the counterfeit Confederates had been unaware of the wagon train's presence, he would know it now. Even as Rait watched, the scouts dropped back, disappeared below the ragged hogback.

He reached the bluff and halted. The area beneath the escarpment was a ledge fifty feet or so in width before it fell away onto a long, running slope that ended in a brush-filled wash far below. Its length was perhaps twice its breadth but with steeper grades leading up from the adjacent swales.

There were a few rocks that could be used in fortifying the small plain; a rim of snakeweed and similar growth, while offering no protection from bullets, would screen the movements of the men. Cook would be forced to make his attack up the hillside under the rifles of the teamsters—at a definite disadvantage—but the rag-tag cavalrymen, by the sheer power of greater numbers, could overrun the rim.

He would have to use the wagons as breastworks, risk damaging some of the cargo. Adam Rait didn't like the thought, but it would be better to lose a few guns than the entire shipment.

He wheeled as Waterhouse's team, mouthing their bits and flecked with lather, pounded onto the level. Rait waved the driver to the far end of the ledge.

"Line up broadside . . . then get the horses back along the foot of the bluff, out of range!" he shouted.

The teamster following Waterhouse heard, swung into place without direction. The third wagon was loaded with ammunition; Rait had it taken to the somewhat lower area where the horses were being picketed. A stray bullet smashing into any one of the wooden cases in its bed could set off an explosion that would end their stand against Cook quickly.

When the last of the vehicles had gained the level and were in position, he had nine lined up in a near solid row across the rim of the ledge, creating an effective bulwark. The remaining three, because of their contents, were parked with the horses and Sancho's chuck wagon.

Adam, brushing sweat and dust from his eyes, rode to the latter position where Sancho and the wrangler were anchoring the last team to a wheel.

"It's up to you to keep the horses in hand," he said, dismounting hastily. "Anything goes wrong, drive them down the far end so's they can run loose."

Turning, he trotted to the center of the flat. Their major weak spot, he judged, was the summit of the cliff towering over them. Cook could send a squad in a wide sweep to approach from the rear. From the rim of the bluff soldiers could pour a murderous fire down upon the teamsters, more or less trapped below.

He beckoned to Earl Handy and Henry Fox. "Get above. Watch for soldiers cutting in on us from behind. You see any signs of that . . . sing out."

The men wheeled, ran toward a slanting fault in the face of the formation that would enable them to climb to the crest.

Gannon came up, sweat soaked and plastered with dust. "You squaring off for a regular war?"

"That's what we're in," Adam snapped.

"Then I reckon you'd better be giving us something to do the fighting with."

Rait said—"Come on."—and, beckoning to several of the crew, crossed to the nearest wagon. Freeing one of the packing cases, he dragged it to the ground. "Give me an axe."

Taking the blade, he pried off the lid, exposed the rifles suspended in layers by notched, wooden crosspieces. Picking up one, he handed it to Gannon. "Pass them around, and break open the ammunition. One thing we don't have to worry about is something to fight with."

Leaving the distribution chore to Gannon, he walked between two of the wagons and halted at the hedge of weeds. Rocks had already been rolled up and put in place, and several of the teamsters were busy digging shallow pits.

Cook and his cavalrymen had still put in no appearance. The Confederate likely was shaping up his formation, planning his strategy. Adam turned to look to the top of the butte. The heads of Fox and Handy were barely visible.

He wished there was some way he could neutralize so weak a spot in their chain of defense, but there was none. He could only hope Zeb Cook would not detect it—at least not until he had made an assault or two from the front and the teamsters had lowered the odds a bit.

He glanced to the southeast. The dust ball that still hung above the horizon was now much larger. He doubted that it was Joe Denver and the boy, Felipe. More than likely it was cattle on the move—or it could be a body of horsemen. He had a faint stir of hope thinking it might be a party of Juáristas patrolling the hills. He shook that off as hardly possible; he was sure they were not that near the border.

He saw two riders topping out a hill a long half mile to the east. Squinting, he studied the figures, something about them being familiar. With a start he recognized Angela and Hernando Bernal. Not quite believing it, he swung his eyes to Sancho and the teams; he had assumed the girl and the Mexican officer would be there, but in the rush to prepare he had not given the matter any thought.

Slowly he turned back. Why had they pulled out on their own? Why hadn't they stayed with the train? For Bernal to abandon his prize, even though the eventual, outcome might be doubtful, made no sense . . . unless . . .

Rait drew himself up sharply, his gaze again on the yellowish cloud. Unless that dust indicated the arrival of Hernando Bernal's Mexican brigade.

That the officer would dare bring his men onto foreign soil, tempt the wrath of the United States, was unbelievable—but he could think of no other answer. And Bernal and those with whom he was allied were desperate, playing for high stakes. The general would take the risk if the results warranted it.

The presence of the Mexican troops was no accident. Thinking back, Adam could see why Bernal had insisted the train turn south—and why Hernando had tried to stop him earlier that evening when he rode out to investigate the dust he thought was being raised by Joe Denver. He figured Rait's curiosity was aroused for an entirely different reason.

It was all a prearranged plan. That accounted for Bernal's supreme confidence in his ability to get the wagon train to Mexico City without difficulty. More than likely the troops had been standing by after having been alerted by Martinez who had continued on across the border after his unsuccessful attempt on Emiliano Escobar's life.

But General Hernando Bernal had not reckoned with the dogged persistence of half-mad Zebulon Cook and his ragged volunteers. He was now faced with but one course of action: hurriedly bring up the Mexican brigade, that was probably not scheduled to enter the picture for another day or so, and protect his prize. He and Angela were moving to join the command at that very moment.

Adam Rait swore grimly. It would develop into a three-way battle—with the teamsters caught in the middle; before it was over, the quiet hills and steep bluffs would witness one hell of a scrap.

Idly he watched the two riders drop from sight behind a hill, and his thoughts settled on Angela. He remembered the way she had looked at him when he rode off to lead the wagons in their hurried flight to the butte. He would not soon forget—and he found himself wishing he had taken time to pause, urge her to join them. Perhaps that would have been the exact moment, the time of truth when she would have made her decision to mesh her life with his.

But he had missed the opportunity, and she had gone her way. It was too late now. That their paths might one day cross again seemed unlikely. Rait stirred impatiently, endeavored to rid himself of the sense of loss that realization engendered—but without success.

Angela could have been his—he knew that now—but he had been pig-headed and insisted that his way was right. What difference did it really make to him who got the shipment of arms—Maximilian or Juárez? Mexico was another land, another world; he could easily spend the rest of his life without setting foot on Mexican soil again.

Yet deep within him he knew that was wrong—that his actions were right, and no amount of self-persuasion would change anything. Conviction, he had learned long ago, was a cruel and costly master, and a man who would live at peace with himself had no choice except to stand firm.

He could solve it all simply by mounting his horse, advising the teamsters to do likewise, and riding off, thus leaving it for pseudo-Colonel Zebulon Cook and Brigade General Hernando Bernal to brawl for the bounty.

But to Adam Rait such a thought was as remote as the yonder edge of infinity.

Chapter Twenty-Three

Again Adam looked to the ridge. Cook was taking his time; if he didn't hurry it would soon be dark. He remembered then the two scouts— they had not returned—which could mean that Cook was intentionally delaying, planning to attack under cover of night. And he could be holding off until morning. . . .

It didn't matter; when it came—it came. The teamsters were as ready as they'd ever be, some of them already crouched behind the wagons, others hunkering in the pits they had dug, or back of the rocks they had piled into small mounds. Adam pulled away from the rim, halted next to the packing case he had removed from one of the wagons. Reaching down, he selected one of the rifles, and then helped himself to a double handful of brass cartridges that he stuffed into his pockets.

He tried the weapon's action, found it smooth. The rifle bore the name of a German manufacturer, looked much like an old Sharps he had once owned, except that it was designed to take the new style ammunition. With such a weapon the teamsters would give a good accounting of themselves—all twenty-one of them, including himself. He grinned bleakly. Twenty-one against fifty, possibly sixty . . . Who the hell was he trying to fool?

But there was one hope he had so far refused to dwell upon: the escort Escobar had promised should be on its way—could even be nearby. If so . . .

A sudden spatter of gunshots broke out in the area beyond the ridge. Adam walked quickly to the edge of the flat. The dust roll he had observed had shifted to the north and was much larger. The riders causing it, he realized, would be some distance on ahead—and that would place them behind the ridge. Bernal's men must have struck.

Another rattle of gunfire, this time prolonged and heavy, echoed flatly across the fading day. Ed Vernon got to his feet, scratched at his whisker-covered jaw, and looked inquiringly at Rait. "Cap'n . . . what the hell's going on?"

"That's your friend Bernal and his soldiers. They've jumped Cook."

"Bernal? Where'd he get soldiers?"

More of the teamsters pulled back from their positions, now stood in silence listening to the distant shooting.

"Had them waiting all the time," Adam replied. "Why do you think he wanted you to head due south for the border?"

Rube Waterhouse leaned his rifle against the wheel of a wagon. "Sure, that's what he told us.

Said he'd have his men take over once we crossed . . . but he didn't say nothing about no soldiers." The man paused, frowned. "We across the border?"

"No, still a few miles away."

"Then what's he bringing in soldiers . . . ?"

"Don't mean nothing, him doing that," Bill Gannon broke in. "I figure he's doing it as a favor . . . sort of protecting us, keeping that Cook off our backs."

Darby Sims said: "Sounds right to me. He just don't want nothing happening to our cargo. Only thing I don't savvy is how come them soldiers of his was so handy?"

Adam Rait only listened. The men were at last realizing the possibility that they might have been duped by the Mexican officer, but were far from convinced. He let it ride. There was nothing that could be done about it now anyway.

The firing beyond the hogback grew in intensity. Smoke, infiltrated by dust, began to hang in a low, bellying cloud above the lengthy formation.

"Sure is a hell of a scrap going on over there," Malachi Lee said. "I'm wondering who's winning?"

"Maybe it don't make no difference," Waterhouse answered. "I'm getting a hunch that Rait's right. Ain't neither one of them fixing to do us no good."

Gannon swore loudly. "And I'm telling you,

you're wrong! The Mex ain't about to pull no double-cross on us. You'll see."

"Liable to be too late . . . when the time comes."

"No it won't! I'm telling you so! And I'll prove it!"

Waterhouse stared at Gannon. "Now, how you aiming to do that? You're the talkingest bastard . . ."

"Just keep your shirt on, I'll prove it."

The shooting began to fade, fell off to a few scattered reports. The huge, ugly cloud was drifting away. Adam glanced to the west. The sun was down, leaving only a flare of reddish gold to mark its passage. There was still time for the victor—whoever it was—to attack the butte.

"Back in your places," he ordered. "Our turn's coming up."

The crew resumed their positions, and a heavy silence, filled with tension, fell over the ledge. But there was no movement on the ridge as darkness, once begun, closed in swiftly. A quarter hour dragged by . . . a half . . .

Rait looked to the men on the summit of the butte. "See anything over there?"

Fox called back: "Nothing 'cept dust and smoke!"

Ed Vernon again arose. "Must've changed their minds, Cap'n."

Bill Gannon laughed. "It's like I was telling you. The general was doing us a favor. He's drove off that crazy bunch of Confederates. Like as not them soldiers of his are headed back for Mexico."

Adam shrugged. He could be wrong since his conclusions had all come from hunches, and the way things had shaped up, but on the other hand Bernal could be playing it cagey; he, too, might be considering a night attack, or a delay until the morning.

"Hope you're right, Bill . . . about all of it," Rait said. "But I'm taking no chances." He turned to Sancho. "Fix some grub, *viejo*. Want to get this eating out of the way."

The cook glanced around. "There is no wood for the fire. It will be difficult."

"Use that box the rifles were in. Dump the rest of those cartridges in a couple of buckets. You'll scrape up enough."

The old man moved off muttering to himself, and Rait swung back to the teamsters. "Have to keep a sharp watch tonight. Figure on three outposts . . . one in front, one at each end of the ledge, two on the rim above us. Four-hour shifts."

"Starting now?" Darby Sims asked.

"It can wait until full dark . . . as long as we all keep an eye on that ridge."

"You picking the sentries?" Gannon wanted to know.

Adam nodded. "I'll have a list ready by the time we're through eating."

He walked to the declivity in the cliff, clawed his way to the top. Handy and Henry Fox greeted him with frowns.

"All that shooting over there . . . what do you figure was going on?" Fox asked.

Rait made his explanation, making clear that it was all assumption on his part and then said: "What I wanted to say was to keep a close watch on the ridge. They could be planning to come at us when it's good and dark."

Earl Handy nodded but it was evident he was not giving it much thought. "What I'm wondering," he said, "is how come that Bernal had soldiers clean up here in the first place."

"The boys are all wondering about that," Adam said, turning for the declivity. "You can hash it over with them when you come down to eat. I'll send up your relief pretty quick."

"Now, hold on a minute," Fox said hurriedly. "You meaning Bernal had them soldiers here, just a-laying for us?"

"It looks that way to me. Expect we'll find out for sure, though, tonight or maybe in the morning."

Handy slammed his hat to the ground angrily. "Why, that god-damned . . ."

"Sure sounds like we've been suckered," Henry Fox murmured. "Should've listened to you, but we was plumb blinded by that extra gold. Anything we can do?"

"Nothing but fight."

"Which bunch you reckon it'll be . . . Cook's or the Mexicans?"

"Bernal is my guess," Adam said, and moved on to the steep path.

Halfway down he heard the thump of Sancho's pounding on the side of his wagon, summoning the men to their meal. He reached the level, accepted a plate of hurriedly prepared, thin stew and warmed-over biscuits, and crossed to one of the wagons where he found a seat on the tongue.

He remembered then the sentry list he had promised and, taking a stub of pencil and a scrap of paper from his pocket, wrote out the names of the men in duty order. It didn't make any difference who stood guard, or when, just so watch was maintained. The roster was completed by the time he had downed his meal, and he turned it over to Ed Vernon.

"I leave it up to you to pass the word. I'll be checking the posts all night."

Vernon signified his understanding, and, list in hand, he began moving among the teamsters, informing them of their shifts.

"Send somebody up to spell off Fox and Handy!" he called after him. "Time they ate."

The night began to brighten as the stars and moon gathered strength. He began to doubt that an attack would be attempted. The engagement beyond the ridge would have taken its toll of men and equipment; Bernal—or Cook—would probably wait until morning, but he would permit no relaxing of the watch.

Shortly before midnight, when he paused at the fire for a cup of Sancho's caustic belly-warmer, he found Vernon, Rube Waterhouse, and Henry Fox there ahead of him.

Waterhouse was sloshing his coffee about in the cup absently. "You figure we got a chance coming out of this, Adam?"

"A slim one," Rait answered.

"Just what we was saying. But if we do . . . ?"

"Somebody's coming!"

The warning came from Red Lester, posted at the south end of the ledge. Adam leaped to his feet, snatching up his rifle.

"Watch close!" he shouted. "They could be moving up!"

"Couple of wagons . . ." Lester's tone was uncertain. "Looks like . . . by hell, it's Joe Denver and the Mex boy!"

Rait cradled his weapon, hurried toward the teamster. He could hear the rattling of the vehicles, the sound broken regularly by shouts from Denver as he urged his team up the slope.

Blocked by the fortifications, he pulled to a stop just below the rim, leaped to the ground, and with Felipe a step behind him legged it for the top.

"What was all that shooting?" he yelled as he came onto the level. "Figured you boys was sure having it hot and heavy."

Adam pointed to the ridge. "Cook and Bernal, fighting it out to see who gets us."

"Who come out on top?"

"Don't know. Expect it was Bernal. From the dust he's got a fair-size army."

Denver glanced appealingly at Sancho, expressing his need for food, then said: "Who's this Bernal?"

Adam frowned, looked closely at the teamster, and then remembered that Joe had missed out on everything that had happened since their parting at the river. He explained in detail while Denver and Felipe satisfied their hunger. When Rait had finished, the driver shook his head, glanced at the dozen or so men who had gathered around.

"We sure've been played for suckers, ain't no doubt of that."

"We ain't giving in yet!" Zeke Kelly declared. "Not by a damn' sight!"

"And we won't," Bill Gannon added. "Can't make nobody see it, but I claim the general's just looking out for us."

Denver stared at the man unbelievingly for a moment, and then glanced around. "Got yourself pretty well forted up here. Be hard for anybody to overrun you, leastwise first couple of times."

"We can hold for a while," Rait said. "I'm hoping that escort from Tupelo heard the shooting and is on its way."

Joe Denver wheeled slowly. "One thing I was aiming to tell you . . . there ain't no escort coming . . . we found Escobar dead first day out."

Chapter Twenty-Four

Rait felt the last measure of hope drain from his body. He had been careful to make no issue of the escort's coming in front of the teamsters, knowing in his own mind there was a strong possibility that it would not; now it was a definite fact. The final mental bulwark with which he restrained despair was gone.

He smiled grimly at Waterhouse. "That slim chance I mentioned . . . you can forget it."

Rube cursed vividly, helplessly. "Well, boys, I reckon that's it."

Denver said: "Any use going for help?"

Adam shook his head. "Too late. It was too late yesterday. As far as I know the nearest town's Tupelo . . . and that's days away."

"Looks like all we can do is fight."

Like a sudden towering wave, the past washed through Adam Rait. It was the war all over again—the same heartbreaking problem that had warped his soul and turned him, blood-sick from the struggle: too few men; overwhelming odds, crisis . . . Stand and die! Revulsion ripped through him. Without conscious thought, he spoke.

"We can quit!"

In the breathless hush that followed, the men stared at him.

"I won't ask you to do this. I want you to understand that. I swore a time ago I'd never again tell a man he had to die. Pick yourself a horse and ride. Head west. Nobody'll stop you."

One-Eye Johnson pulled off his hat angrily. "You meaning . . . just run, leave everything?"

"Is it worth throwing your life away for? That's the price you'll pay if you don't."

Johnson tugged at his stringy mustache. "Could be . . . howsomever, I ain't thinking much on that. It's just the giving up, letting them take what ain't theirs."

"He's right," Kiowa Jack said, bobbing his head. "Reckon I'd rather fight."

Adam wiped at the sweat on his face. He thought back to the times in the swamps of Tennessee, to the hills of Virginia, of Pennsylvania—and a half a hundred other skirmishes in long-forgotten places. Except for the lack of uniforms, this could be one of those instances unfolding before him again.

"We ain't about to go hightailing it, Cap'n," Ed Vernon said quietly. "Not even if that Bernal's got hisself two hundred soldiers over there."

Adam Rait heard, and began to realize that those men who had stood by him in the tumultuous, smoky days of the war, who had faced crushing odds, just as these, had felt the same way.

They, too, had declined to run. And while, as their commanding officer, he could have made no such offer as that which he presented to the teamsters, he knew now they, too, would have refused. Life was precious, but to brave men defending what they believed to be right, it was not the ultimate to be preserved above all else.

He became aware of a curious lifting of spirit, and somewhere in the back recesses of his mind a dark shadow dissolved. It was strange that it had taken so long to find the answer, stranger yet to meet it on a sandy ledge in Texas, far from the battlefields where it all began—and in the face of certain death.

A pride swelled through him and his shoulders came up a notch. "All right. That's the way it'll be. We'll give them holy hell long as we last."

There was no cheering this time, only a quiet assent.

"I know you're all set," Rait continued. "But you might keep an extra rifle handy in case the one you're using blows up. Be sure you've got plenty of cartridges. Men not on sentry duty ought to get some sleep."

The men nodded and moved off. Adam, with Denver, dropped back to the end of the ledge. Together they cleared the way and brought in the horses and wagons the teamster and Felipe had abandoned outside camp.

When that was done, Denver said: "About time

you was taking some of your own advice and getting some shut-eye. You look like a walking dead man. I'll have the boy fix you a bed in the wagon."

Rait heaved a sigh, suddenly conscious of weariness. "I'll do that . . . soon as I look things over."

"I'll do the looking over," the teamster said firmly. "You're hitting the hay."

Adam grinned, stood by while Felipe spread blankets in the supply wagon, and then crawled aboard.

"Couple of hours," he murmured. "That's all I'll need."

"Sure . . . couple of hours," Joe Denver answered.

Chapter Twenty-Five

The next thing Rait knew someone was shaking him by the shoulder. He sat bolt upright, alarm racing through him. It was first light, and Denver, a dim figure at the end of the wagon, was staring at him.

"Better have a look," the teamster boss said. "We got Mexicans all over that slope."

Adam flung aside the blankets, cursing himself for having slept so long, and leaped to the ground. He cast a hasty glance around the ledge. The men were in their places. Sancho and Felipe had coffee boiling over the fire and were preparing the morning meal.

At a trot he crossed to the edge of the flat, made his way between two of the freighters, and halted. Ed Vernon, hunched in his pit, looked up.

"Must be a hundred of them, Cap'n, at least."

Rait scanned the distant hillside below the ridge. Bernal had won the fight with Cook, as he had expected, and now had moved his forces into view. It was too dark for an accurate estimate but he guessed Vernon's count was low.

Slowly the hills lightened as the sun crept nearer to the horizon in the east. Dim shapes began to take definite form: the soldiers wore blue uniforms. These were Maximilian's best—expertly trained and well armed. He stirred impatiently. How long did he think he could hold them off with a dozen and a half riflemen?

Felipe sounded the call to breakfast. The teamsters collected immediately, sensing the need to hurry, bolted their meal. The two men on the summit of the bluff were relieved and sentries along the edge of the flat came in.

Darby Sims, swallowing the last of his coffee, moved up to where Bill Gannon stood. "Expect you're changing your mind now about that son-of-a-bitching Mex!"

"No, I ain't! Still figure he's for us. Aim to ride over there in a minute and prove it."

Rait looked up sharply. "Don't be a fool, Bill."

The teamster snorted. "I'll show you who's the fool!" he shouted, and, throwing his plate to the ground, he strode to the horses. Choosing one, he drew on a bridle and, ignoring the use of a saddle, vaulted into position.

"Be right back. You'll see!"

Denver, standing beside Rait, clucked softly as he watched the teamster diminish into the distance. "Got me a hunch old Bill's done his last talking."

The men stood in silence, eyes on the slope. Gannon reached the welter of blue uniforms and, unchallenged, walked his mount toward the center. Abruptly he was lost to sight.

Rait glanced around, habit compelling him to

make a final inspection. Hernando Bernal would not delay much longer. His men, too, would have had their rations, soon would be forming ranks. The classic cavalry charge, he guessed, would be the officer's plan. Send several waves of men pounding up the slope and overrun the opposition by sheer force of numbers.

A gunshot racketed hollowly across the stillness. Adam wheeled. Bill Gannon, crouched low on his horse, was rushing downgrade. There was a confused milling about among the soldiers, and then a small space along the edge cleared. A half dozen men formed a line. Rifles echoed.

Gannon raised himself slightly and sagged to one side. The guns blasted again. Horse and rider disappeared into a turmoil of dust as both went down.

"They got him," Red Lester muttered. "The dirty, stinking . . ."

"Was a fool thing he done," Malachi Lee cut in. "He know'd better . . . just couldn't stand being showed up wrong."

"Proves you knew what you was talking about, Cap'n," Vernon said. "Can't be no doubt now."

Adam felt no elation, no sense of triumph. Bill Gannon had simply believed himself right; it had cost him his life to learn the opposite was true and that Hernando Bernal was a man not to be trusted.

"Cap'n."

It was Ed Vernon again. The teamster was pointing down the slope. The Mexican officer was sending a party to negotiate. Hanging his rifle in the crook of his arm, Rait stepped over the rim of weeds and rock, took up a stand a few paces below. The four men advancing immediately halted.

"Do you speak Spanish?" the officer in the lead called.

"I know the tongue," Adam replied.

"General Bernal sends this message. He will spare the lives of you and your men. It is only necessary that you remove yourself from your position and walk to us. Horses will later be provided for your convenience."

Rait thought of Bill Gannon. "Your general is not to be trusted. He would have bullets put into our backs as he did the man who went to speak with him."

"An assassin," the officer replied. "He became angered, endeavored to murder General Bernal . . . who did sustain a slight wound. Such treachery was necessarily rewarded with death."

It was not difficult now to understand what had happened. Bernal had told Bill Gannon the truth, and the teamster, in a fit of rage, had shot the officer.

"What is your answer?"

"Tell your general he can go to hell," Rait said, forgetting his Spanish. "And he can look for . . ."

"I do not understand."

"The offer is refused."

"An unwise decision. You have no more than two dozen men. Perhaps less. Against them we will mount four times that number."

"Hey, who's that coming?"

Adam turned, followed the teamster's gaze. A number of riders, strung out in a short line, were galloping across the swale for the south end of the butte. They were following the tracks made earlier by Denver and Felipe. There were nine horses in the party and all except the one in the lead were carrying double.

"Juáristas!" Joe Denver shouted. "Sure as the devil!"

"That the escort we're waiting for?" Waterhouse asked.

Rait moved back to the ledge. "Couldn't be. Nobody knows we're here."

"Well, they sure do!"

The oncoming riders became more distinct. They wore large sombreros, and now and then the growing light glinted off rifles carried by some of the men. The men riding double appeared to be unarmed. And the one in the lead . . . there was something familiar . . .

"It's that gal!" Kiowa Jack Green said, using his hand as a visor. "The one that was with the Mex general. By doggies, she's a bringing us some help!"

Adam could scarcely believe his eyes, and unconsciously his guard came up as suspicion claimed him. But he wasted no time in thought. Throwing a glance at Bernal's negotiating party, now loping back to the slope to make their report, he swung his attention to the teamsters.

"Hold your positions until I see what this iS all about," he said, and hurried into the center of the ledge. He beckoned to Denver. "Joe. Give me a hand here," he said, and rushed on to the lower end of the plain to make an entrance for the riders.

With the additional help of Sancho and the wrangler, they hustled the supply rig to one side. Moments later Angela de Acera, followed by the others, poured through the gap and came to a halt.

Adam stepped to the girl's winded horse, helped her dismount. She smiled, made a gesture toward the men coming off their mounts.

"Sixteen men . . . all I could find."

Still mystified, Rait looked at the Mexicans, spun to Joe Denver. "Get them armed . . . those that need guns. Find them places along the rim."

The teamster beckoned to the men, trotted off. Frowning, Rait followed them with his eyes.

"All loyal Juáristas," Angela said, reading his mind. "It's no trick."

He turned to her. Her face was smudged with

dust, and a fine film covered her clothing. She had evidently ridden long and hard.

"Juáristas," he echoed. "What are you doing with the Juáristas?"

Angela smiled again. "I've never been anything else," she said.

Chapter Twenty-Six

Adam Rait, vaguely angered, said nothing.

"I tried to make you understand without actually telling you," Angela said. "But I was afraid someone might hear and it would get back to Bernal."

He nodded slowly. "You're a Juárez agent, but you let the Maximilian bunch think you were with them. And all that about Mexico City . . . and other things."

"It's true, most of it. I'll admit some of it was just conversation . . . just so I could be with you. My father is a *grandee*, except he's one of the few who believes in Benito Juárez. Secretly, of course. It was easy for us to listen and watch, keep Juárez posted."

"That doesn't explain why you were after Hanover and the shipment of arms."

"That came about accidentally. When word was received at the palace that Hanover was arriving with a cargo of guns, Maximilian's advisers decided Bernal would be sent to get them . . . one way or another. Somebody got the idea that Hanover might be easier to deal with if a woman was brought in on the scheme. He was, they said, quite a ladies' man."

"So they picked you."

She studied him closely, intrigued by the sharp quality of his tone. Amusement flickered in her eyes. "I was never in any danger from him."

Rait looked toward the slope. The mass of blue-clad cavalrymen had not moved.

"Anyway, being chosen was just what I hoped for," she continued. "Maximilian's generals have had a troop of soldiers hiding out along the border, near here, for a long time. They've caused Juárez a lot of trouble raiding villages, destroying supply trains, capturing messengers, and the like."

"I've heard of them," Adam said. "Nobody could ever figure out where they holed up." He hesitated, frowned. "That's probably the same bunch Bernal's got with him now."

"It is. We were sure he'd visit them, or drop a word that would tell me where they were, so I agreed to accompany him. All I was interested in was finding out the location of the secret rendezvous . . . and then getting word to Juárez so it could be destroyed."

"Did you?"

Angela nodded. "Last night. As soon as I was sure, I slipped off, rode to a village south of here, looking for help. I was lucky a Juárista patrol was there. I sent one man on to Tupelo with a map for the *comandante*, and talked the rest . . . eight men . . . into coming with me to help you. They recruited eight of the villagers.

Now that you have sixteen more to fight, do you think . . . ?"

Rait's features softened. He reached for her, drew her close. "You've been taking a hell of a lot of chances . . . and you shouldn't have come here. Not much hope for us. . . ."

"I wanted to come. I had to be with you."

"Adam!"

Joe Denver's summons brought him around quickly. The blue mass on the distant slope had begun to flow downward. Taking Angela by the shoulders, he kissed her firmly, turned her about, and pushed her toward Sancho and the safety at the foot of the bluff. "Stay over there. If we come through this alive, we've got some plans to make," he said, and hurried away.

Rifle in hand, he halted at center front of the ledge, ran his gaze along the line of crouched men fanning out to either side. Several of the newcomers grinned back, teeth showing whitely in their dark faces. The odds now were considerably better—but still not good.

He threw his attention to the slope. Bernal, carrying a saber, had reached the bottom and had halted in the wash. His men were spreading out to form lines. Methodically Adam made a count: five rows of horsemen, twenty in each except for the last, which contained twenty-four.

Hernando's plan was apparent. The first row would be the shock troops, designed to draw the teamsters' initial fire. They would be followed closely by the second wave whose jobs it would be to race in on the heels of the leading cavalry-men, get their licks in before reloading on the part of the teamsters could be completed. The third, fourth, and fifth lines would serve mostly in the capacity of mopping up.

It was standard procedure, and under ordinary circumstances usually effective. But like most officers who went strictly by the book, Bernal was misjudging the situation, convinced he would have little difficulty in overpowering so small an enemy.

Not only was he ignoring the disadvantage of charging an opponent entrenched on higher ground, but he was also failing to reckon with the firepower of the improved rifles being used by Rait and his men.

Adam watched the forming ranks in silence. After the first wave struck, he would have some idea of their chances. Until then he could only hope. He swept the teamsters and their reinforcements with a final glance; there was no conversation, only a complete hush. Below, in the wash a bugle sounded. Hammers clicked along the ridge as rifles were cocked.

"Here they come," someone said quietly.

"Hold your fire until they're in range," Adam warned.

Malachi Lee lazily turned half around. "Now,

how'll we be knowing when that is?" he drawled. "Ain't none of us ever fired one of these new-fangled irons."

"That hump of rocks and weeds," Rait said, pointing to a rise some fifty yards below. "That's your deadline." He repeated his words in Spanish for benefit of the Juáristas.

"Ain't that a mite close?" Darby Sims wondered.

"It's this first round that'll count," Adam replied.

The bugle blared louder, slicing through a burst of yelling. The first wave of cavalrymen hit the bottom of the near slope, started up. The shouts increased and scattered shooting began as the line of horsemen began to break its exact regularity on the rough grade.

"Wait," Adam cautioned.

The cavalry thundered on, dust now churning up in boiling clouds. Off to the left Rait could see Bernal, saber swinging overhead, whipping back and forth.

"Fire!"

He gave the order the exact instant the riders reached the clump. Immediately gunshots echoed deafeningly along the line of wagons. Half the riders in the first wave buckled in their saddles. Several fell to the ground, bounced limply, and lay still. Others, clawing at leather, curved off to make way for the second line.

The follow-up troopers did not withhold their

fire; they opened up immediately. Bullets thudded dully into the wagons, sang off the iron tires, ricocheted against the rocks. Ben Tipton muttered a curse, fell back, plainly dead. Gunshots continued to crackle steadily from the rim. More cavalry-men sagged, fell, or wheeled off clutching their wounds.

Hernando Bernal had halted and was staring up the slope. He appeared startled, but he did nothing to stop the third wave of charging soldiers now rushing into the merciless blast of the teamsters' guns.

Adam, firing mechanically, peered through the layers of dust and smoke drifting across the hillside, waited for the sound of the bugle to call retreat. Surely Hernando Bernal would not be fool enough to keep coming.

But the wave closed. The guns of the teamsters crackled again, drowning the reports of the troopers' weapons. More cavalrymen wilted, fell away. And two more of the crouched drivers jerked back, cursing. The one to Adam's left— Jules Bundy—continued to swear in a steady monotone as he sought to stuff his bandana into a fountain of blood in his groin. The other man, facedown, lay quiet.

And then the bugle's shrill notes rolled out over the hillside, echoed against the butte. Bernal had decided to withdraw. Rait could see the shadowy figures of cavalrymen cutting about in the haze, starting down the slope. Yells went up from the teamsters. Adam turned slowly, looked toward the horses. Angela was all right.

"Is that Larsen, lying there with his head shot off?"

Someone moved past him, stepped to the teamster lying facedown, and rolled him onto his back. It was Larsen; a bullet had caught him in the forehead. Rait began to check further. Four more dead: Oliver Cook, old Malachi Lee, and two of the Mexican recruits. There were three wounded, including Bundy. They had done well, exacting a penalty of four or five to one from the ranks of Bernal's Imperial Guards. Adam's hopes began to lift.

"Here they come again!"

Rait whirled. The Mexican officer had changed his tactics. No longer was he hurling his entire command straight up the front slope. Instead, he had thrown them out in a wide line and was approaching the fortifications on the ledge from all three sides.

"Spread out!" Adam yelled, seizing some of the men by the shoulder, pushing them toward the ends of the flat where their concentration was thinnest.

The line of blue surged up the slopes, the expertness of their training evident in the almost perfect shoulder-to-shoulder formation they maintained.

"Hold for my signal!" Rait shouted.

His judgment must be right, he knew. Unless Bernal's men were met with a concentrated fire at just the correct moment, the ends of the teamsters' line of fortifications, far weaker than the center, would be quickly overrun.

He waited, trying to see through the dust. Straining, he saw the first of the line reach the marker he had earlier employed on the front slope. Raising his rifle, he counted off ten seconds.

"Fire!"

All along the grade that flowed from the butte the line of blue faltered. Men yelled in pain, horses went down, thrashing wildly. A few answering shots sounded but they were a weak response to the steady, rapid shooting of the teamsters and the Juáristas, now accustomed to their new weapons.

Rait peered into the rolling clouds of smoke and dust. He could not locate Bernal, could see only bodies littering the three sides of the slope. The firing dwindled and came to a halt. Slowly the thick haze drifted away. A yell went up from the teamsters. The assault had failed again; Hernando Bernal's cavalrymen were gathering in the sandy wash once more.

"You reckon that's it, Cap'n?" Ed Vernon called from the far end of the ledge.

"Stay where you are!" Rait answered quickly. The general could make another final, desperate attempt. He glanced toward the wagons. Angela and Sancho were busy with the wounded. He wondered how many more had fallen. He had seen only one man stumble and fall—Kiowa Jack, he thought.

Activity in the wash caught his attention. Three soldiers, one bearing a white flag, rode forward, halted a few yards up the slope.

"We withdraw!" the officer in the group shouted. "With your permission we will gather our dead and wounded."

Adam moved to the edge of the flat. He pointed to the cavalrymen, mounted and waiting. "Order your men to retreat. Then you may proceed."

The officer turned, gave a command. The troopers, with the exception of those delegated to assist in the grisly recovery, wheeled and slanted across the wash for the distant hillside.

Those remaining began to climb the slopes. They first loaded the wounded onto their horses, sent them to where the cavalrymen were assembling. When that was done, they collected the dead, draping the bodies over saddles, lashing hands and feet together to hold them secure.

General Hernando Bernal was one of those. . . .

About the Author

Ray Hogan was an author who inspired a loyal following over the years since he published his first Western novel, *Ex-Marshal*, in 1956. Hogan was born in Willow Springs, Missouri, where his father was town marshal. At five the Hogan family moved to Albuquerque where they lived in the foothills of the Sandia and Manzano Mountains. His father was on the Albuquerque police force and, in later years, owned the Overland Hotel. It was while listening to his father and other old-timers tell tales from the past that Ray was inspired to recast these tales in fiction. From the beginning he did exhaustive research into the history and the people of the Old West, and the walls of his study were lined with various firearms, spurs, pictures, books, and memorabilia, about all of which he could talk in dramatic detail. "I've attempted to capture the courage and bravery of those men and women that lived out West and the dangers and problems they had to overcome," Hogan once remarked. If his lawmen protagonists seem sometimes larger than life, it is because they are men of integrity, heroes who through grit of character and common sense are able to overcome the obstacles they encounter despite often overwhelming odds. This same grit of character can also be found in Hogan's heroines, and in *The Vengeance of Fortuna West* (1983) Hogan wrote a gripping and totally believable account of a woman who takes up the badge and tracks the men who killed her lawman husband by ambush. No less intriguing in her way is Nellie Dupray, convicted of rustling in *The Glory Trail* (1978). One of his most popular books, dealing with an earlier period in the West with Kit Carson as its protagonist, is *Soldier in Buckskin* (1996). Above all, what is most impressive about Hogan's Western novels is the consistent quality with which each is crafted, the compelling depth of his characters, and his ability to juxtapose the complexities of human conflict into narratives always as intensely interesting as they are emotionally involving.

Center Point Large Print
600 Brooks Road / PO Box 1
Thorndike, ME 04986-0001 USA

(207) 568-3717

US & Canada:
1 800 929-9108
www.centerpointlargeprint.com